Just Friends

#JustFriends Series - Book 1

MARIE COLE

To WA, I don't think I would have had the ability to do this without you. Thank you.

Just Friends

Chapter 1

Fall 2002 - Junior Year

I glanced around the crowded apartment nervously. Over the summer I'd lost forty of the last seventy-five extra pounds I'd been carrying around with me for most of my adolescent life. I had yet to show anyone, save for my grandmother, whom I'd spent the summer with.

Before leaving the dorm, I'd made sure my new dark wash boot-cut jeans hugged my curves tightly and that the black corset did its job in making my boobs, smaller than average, look hot. But halfway to the party my palms started to sweat. I still wasn't used to having this tiny body. And I wasn't ready for the amount of questions I was going to receive, especially from my skinny acquaintances who were going to want to know my secret, even though they didn't need to know. And it wasn't a secret at all.

Maybe this was a mistake. Maybe I shouldn't be showing off just yet. They'd all see me when I returned to classes in a few days and I wasn't really ready to face Kent and Jen. Jen especially. She was going to rub it in my face that she was still with him and I wasn't.

I was about to turn around when a car passed by and honked at me. I braced myself for the usual insult to follow but instead the college guy yelled, "Hey baby!" It was the confidence boost I needed to keep going.

Three steps into the party and I was assaulted with greetings and compliments. I smiled politely and accepted them, but I was distracted, searching for a certain someone.

I scanned the room, looking for my best friend, wondering how Kent would react now that his long-time BFF was not fat or just average but finally super-hot. He probably wouldn't even notice but I was eager to find out just the same.

I couldn't help the smile that broke out on my face at the sight of him, moving back and forth on his feet, chatting amongst a group of guys. It looked like all the working out he'd been doing was treating him rather well, the blue and white plaid button down he was wearing stretched across his wide chest and larger than average biceps.

It also appeared he'd had surgery or perhaps he was wearing contacts because those thick glasses that I'd loved so much weren't perched on his nose. I wouldn't have recognized him if it hadn't been for his uncomfortable expression as he stood amongst the sea of people. I knew that I'd get over his way eventually and didn't rush it. I didn't want to seem over-eager to see him. I had to play it cool. That's what hot girls did, wasn't it?

I kept glancing in his direction though, to make sure I didn't lose him, and to see what his face was going to give away the moment he caught sight of my new and improved body.

Kent wasn't looking around much, but one of the guys he was talking to actually pointed at me. Kent followed the guy's finger towards me. He stared at me for a long moment as if trying to solve the puzzle that was the smokin' hot me. He blinked a few times and I swear I saw his lips mutter "holy shit" before his lips broke into a warm smile. The guy who had pointed me out elbowed Kent and nodded with his head in my direction. Kent nodded, went to push up the glasses that weren't on his face and ran his hand through his hair instead.

Smooth.

I grinned before looking back to my freshman roommate who was chatting with me about her summer spent in Venice. I was a little jealous hearing about how gorgeous it was but also a little distracted. I was replaying Kent's reaction in my head over and over. Maybe junior year would be my year. Maybe I would finally have the guts to tell him how I felt, how I'd been feeling since middle school. And maybe, just maybe he'd finally see me as a girl, and not just as a pal.

Ever since Jen's arrival to our little high school four years ago Kent and I had started to drift apart. She's set her sights on him and he'd gone along with it. Not that I could blame him for wanting the tall, blonde, skinny cheerleader type. She was nice too, to everyone except me, that is.

As Kent broke away from his group of guys Jen intercepted him, intertwining her fingers with his. He gazed lovingly at Jen and offered her a smile. Kent must have been talking about me because he pointed at me near the end of whatever it was he was saying. I quickly looked away and pretended I wasn't watching them. Suddenly I felt extremely self-conscious and the urge to run like a serial killer was on my tail grew stronger.

I forced those feelings away and turned and smiled at them both after saying parting words to my friend. My eyes found, first Kent, my smile not nearly as warm as before, and then Jen.

"Hey guys!", "I barely recognized him without his glasses." I pointed at Kent, but spoke to Jen. I didn't feel comfortable giving Kent a direct compliment so I had to refer to him in third person, to his girlfriend, right in front of him. Jen had a way of making me feel as if I threatened her relationship that she was going to utterly destroy my entire existence. It was pretty scary in high school, especially with me being the fat girl and her being the rich, popular new girl.

Jen grinned as she moved over and gave me a big hug. "I know. I told him he shouldn't have because the glasses added character."

Kent shook his head. "You didn't have to wear the glasses, Jen." He sounded slightly annoyed, but it soon faded as he looked at me. "You look good, Elly."

I nodded as I looked at him. I looked good. Good? Was that

good or bad? Average? Did he notice my boobs in this top?

Kent didn't get to say any more because Jen followed right after him. "Yeah, Elly. You look amazing. Did you lose like a hundred pounds or something? I can actually see your collarbones." Jen was trying to be nice in her way, which wasn't very. She reached out and traced the bones that were once hidden by fat.

I shrugged off the sting of her words after briefly looking over Kent's hardened form. God how I itched to reach out and touch him. His biceps looked much bigger than they had last Thanksgiving when I'd seen him. But I knew that would be an unwelcome touch and completely inappropriate given that his girlfriend was standing right next to him.

I swallowed back my lusty feelings and forced my smile a little brighter as I clenched my fists and crossed them over my chest, tucking them into my elbows to try to hide the possible give-away that I wanted to punch Jen in her pretty face. "Yeah... So, are you guys on-campus or off-campus this year? I'm on-campus in the Goodman dorm. A single. I was so stoked when I got my letter this summer."

Kent shook his head and smiled just enough to erase the frown off his face. "I'm on-campus in a triple and Jen is off-campus."

Jen was smiling, probably reveling in the fact that her parents could afford to house her off-campus while the rest of us had to man up and live like poor college students we were.

I smiled, trying to make it as genuine as possible. "That's great! Which apartment building?" I could see that Kent was about to speak but Jen butted in.

"I'm just off Polk Street like a hundred feet from campus."

"That's so great! I'd love to come by and see it sometime. If I'm invited, of course." I inwardly cursed myself as I glanced between them. I hadn't wanted to look at him! But it was done now and I wasn't sure if I was relieved to see that he didn't look very happy or not. It was probably just because Jen was taking over the conversation.

Jen smiled and nodded. "Yeah, I know Kent is officially in the dorms this year but I'm sure he'll be over all the time. He has his own dresser and everything. And we stay pretty busy, but I'm sure we can find time to have you over."

"Well...that would be great." Another friend of mine grabbed my elbow and smiled, letting me know she wanted to chat. I looked at Kent and Jen and smiled, pointing over my shoulder. "I should go. It was great seeing you guys, though. Call me, Jen, and let me know when I can get the tour." I smiled and then waved at them.

I didn't give them a chance for much of a goodbye before my friend was looking over me and screaming, "Oh my god! You look great! I hardly recognized you! What's your secret?!"

Chapter 2

The following morning I was at the gym, I spotted a guy coming towards the treadmills. He was tall, had blonde shaggy hair, and light colored eyes. He moved up the two stairs to the platform that all the cardio equipment sat on. I saw the top of his shoe drag on the step and take him down out of the corner of my eye. He slid on his elbows right behind my machine. I gasped and turned it off. I turned around as he was pushing off the ground, noting his sleek back muscles just before he stood up and smiled. He held up his elbow to examine the rubber burn.

His eyes were hazel and he smiled when they found mine. "Do you have a Band-Aid? Because I just scraped my elbow falling for you."

I couldn't help it, I bust out laughing. "Does that really work?"

He grinned and shrugged his broad shoulders, which glistened with sweat under his gray tank top. "We'll see in a few minutes. I'd like to get to know you." He waggled his eyebrows and I scoffed, grinning.

"Wow. I think you need to work on your lines a little more." I turned around and started my treadmill again.

"Kyle." He stepped up onto the treadmill next to mine and started running.

"What?" I turned my head to look at him with raised eyebrows.

"My name...it's Kyle." He leaned his head over towards me and spoke softly, "This is the part where you tell me your name."

"Elly." I closed my eyes and shook my head. I had no idea why I had told him my name, my real name, anyway. "Is this the part where you tell me how you lost your phone number and ask if you can have mine?"

"Oooh, that's a good one. But no, I was going ask you if you sat in a pile of sugar...because you have a pretty sweet ass."

I gasped, mouth open wide, grinning.

He winked. "I have lots of cheesy lines, it's not how I usually do things. I just thought you might appreciate them."

I smiled, I couldn't help it. The guy was gorgeous, funny, a little goofy and he was talking to me.

"God, your smile is beautiful." He looked at his treadmill. "I need to stop staring or I'm going to crash or some shit."

I actually had a whole brain full of cheesy pick-up lines thanks to the silly role-playing I used to do with Kent when we were younger, where we'd practice hitting on each other. It was never a successful venture. We always ended up laughing. "You know, I was feeling a little off today but you turned me on," I said.

He chuckled and retorted, "I'm sorry, I don't think we've met. I wouldn't forget a pretty face like that."

"You know... you look so familiar; didn't we have class together? I could've sworn we had chemistry." I grinned and wondered if this was going to be our thing twenty years from now.

He smiled back and without flinching he stared into my eyes, "You're so beautiful that you made me forget my pick-up line..." He cleared his throat and looked back to his screen. "Say you'll have dinner with me."

"Oooh, it's just too much pressure." I shook my head no.

"Come on, say you will. Don't make me run at super-fast speed just to impress you."

I raised my eyebrows, intrigued. "Well, now I think you definitely have to."

He groaned. "Okay, if I must." His machine beeped as he hit the up arrow several times. The machine whirred to life, the high-pitched sound interrupted by his footfalls as he ran faster and faster. I watched and covered my mouth with my hand, genuinely impressed that he was hanging in there.

The sweat started to bead on his forehead and his breath was rapidly increasing. I wasn't sure how much longer he was going to be able to hold out so I pulled his emergency stop, "Okay! I'll have dinner with you." I grinned as he pulled up his shirt to wipe the sweat from his face, revealing his defined abs. I was drooling and barely shut my mouth before he pulled his shirt back down. We exchanged numbers and made plans for the next evening.

* * *

He convinced me to go over to his place for pizza and a movie. Private time alone with Mr. Kyle McAbs was not against my overall plan to get a boyfriend so that I could stop thinking about my unavailable best friend, so I agreed.

He was in the dorm across campus and he also had a single. I walked down the hallway past freshmen guys who were still getting used to being the small fish in the big pond again, and grinned as they hooted and made comments. I was still very much enjoying the attention so I smiled to myself but didn't otherwise acknowledge them.

I knocked on Kyle's door and heard a little shuffling. The doorknob turned and the door swung open revealing a tidy room with lowered lighting. His eyes raked over my body before he stepped aside and motioned with his hand to the inside of the room.

"Elly, you look...amazing. Come on in."

"Thanks." I stepped in and looked around, taking note of his black bedspread, his magazine files for each of his classes, the tiny TV set on the dresser parallel to the bed. "So this is it, huh?"

He stepped up beside me, nodded, and looked around as if taking it in for the first time. "Yep, this is it. The pizza should be here any minute. Do you want to sit down?" He motioned to his bed with an outstretched arm. I sat down on his bed, probably looking every bit as uncomfortable as I felt. "So I've got two movies to choose from, Vanilla Sky with Cameron Diaz and Tom Cruise or Zoolander with Ben Stiller." He held them up for me to glance at briefly before setting them down on the bed next to me.

"Um...Vanilla Sky," I said, pointing to it. He popped it in and then sat down next to me, his hand right next to mine on the bed.

Ten minutes into the movie he got up and laid down behind me on his side. He ran his hand slowly up my back causing my center to melt. "Lay back, relax. I won't bite unless you ask me to."

I chuckled and slipped off my shoes before laying down in front of him. He spooned me and I felt his hand on my hip, his hot breath on my ear as he watched the movie with a hand propping up his head.

Half an hour into the movie his hand, which had been so innocently resting on my hip, started to slide forward onto my stomach under my shirt. I felt my side seize up, and I giggled, discovering that I was ticklish there.

I grabbed his hand and put it back onto my hip. I didn't turn to look back at him, but I sensed he felt a little put off. He kissed my cheek and then disappeared for a few minutes. When he came back he tried again but instead of his hand moving over my stomach it went for my chest. As his lips pressed against my neck I felt my back arch and I pressed my breast into his hand. He squeezed it softly as he kissed his way to my mouth.

It felt like his hands were everywhere at once. I had no idea what to do with my hands. Did I put them on his back or on his face? I wasn't sure so they laid limp on either side of my head against the pillow. I felt the heat and liquid gather between my legs as he continued to kiss and fondle me and when his hand cupped me through my jeans I bucked my hips and moaned. Woah! Who knew touching could feel so good?

He groaned as his hands then moved to my jeans, undoing the front of them quickly and then his own. "Oh baby, you're so fucking hot."

I lifted my hips when he pulled on my jeans, still unsure of what was going to happen. He tugged them down and then off, letting them fall onto the floor. He stood at the end of his bed as he discarded his own, revealing his plain white boxers. He was straining against the fabric.

I was curious about what it looked like but I didn't want him to feel self-conscious with this girl staring at his penis so I forced my eyes up to his face. His eyes were focused on my panties. For a moment, I was worried that he didn't like them but he seemed concerned only with getting them off of me as was evidenced by his quick hands.

Once my panties were off his boxers were next, and before I could blink again he was on top of me. He was kissing me, then he slid his tip through my wetness and slowly slipped it inside. I felt the heat in my face and stayed still beneath him not sure what was going on. I kept my eyes closed, and wondered, briefly, where the pizza was. And how long sex usually took. And when it was supposed to be good.

He pulled back and reached into his bedside table drawer pulling out a condom. I heard the rip as the plastic made way for the rubber. He slid it on slowly, allowing me a look at his penis and then resumed his position. "You're so hot, baby..." He pushed forward, slipping into my tightness, he felt a little resistance but didn't stop, instead he thrust through and I bit my lower lip as I cried out.

"Fuck!" He groaned still going painfully slowly, I felt the ache start to dull down and soon I wanted him moving.

"Please," I begged softly and his hips started to move spastically. His bit on his lower lip and threw his head back.

"I can't...I can't...FUCK!" He shouted at the same moment that he came inside me, I guessed. I didn't feel anything but he retreated and then left to go clean up in the bathroom leaving me alone. I felt like I had been split between my thighs. I rolled off the bed and slipped my clothes back on. The end credits weren't even rolling yet but I was ready to go.

I wasn't sure if he realized he'd just taken my virginity, but surely if he did, he knew he was being a dick right now. Or was he? Maybe he was giving me privacy so that I could clean up or cry or leave or all of the above. I wasn't going to stick around to ask him. I frowned as I left his room, the asshole took my virginity and didn't even buy me dinner first.

I wouldn't be so stupid the next time a man flashed his cute smile my way.

Chapter 3

After I showered to wash away the shame, I called my old roommate, Stacy, and asked her to meet me at the gym. I had to tell someone what had happened and I knew she would keep it to herself.

She was already waiting outside as I arrived and I hooked my arm in hers as I pulled her inside with me.

The gym was empty around the cardio equipment. Just mirrors and TVs to greet us. There were free weights on the other side of the mirrored walls, but no one ever used those. And if they were being used you could usually tell by all the grunting and man noises.

"Thanks for meeting me," I said as we made our way to the stair-climbers. I was still very sore from losing my V-card, but I was hoping that the self-induced burning in my legs would take my mind off of it.

"Sure thing, thanks for saving me from eating a whole pizza by myself," she grinned as she stepped on the machine beside me.

"Anytime. So…" I sighed and shook my head. I started slow on the machine, wincing a little.

"So…" She waited for me to begin.

"I met this guy at the g—" I stopped myself and looked around in case he was here. I looked back at Stacy, no sign of Kyle. "At the gym. God, he was so cute and funny."

Stacy nodded as she listened, her eyes on me.

"And you know, I've been so hung up on you-know-who and so ashamed of my body that I didn't date or anything. Well…" I let my words trail off as I watched Stacy's eyes widen.

"You went on a date?!" She sounded so thrilled for me. I hated to have to burst her happy bubble but this wasn't what the meeting was about.

I nodded slowly and sucked in my lower lip. "Yes...kind of," I groaned and shook my head in shame.

"Kind of? How can you kind of go on a date?" Her shoulders drooped. "Oh God! Did he take you to McDonald's or something?"

"I think a date at McDonald's would've been better."

Stacy's eyes widened more and I was worried that they might pop out of her head. "Well don't keep me waiting." Her climbing grew faster to match her anticipation.

"Sorry. He invited me over to his dorm. And when I got there he told me that he'd ordered pizza and that we could watch a movie while we waited for it to come."

"Okay," she sounded apprehensive.

"Well, so I picked Vanilla Sky and we were sitting on his bed. He was rubbing my back and stuff. It was nice. And then he laid down behind me and pulled me down next to him. His hand went to my hip and then it started to slide under my shirt. Are you really ticklish there?"

She thought about it for a second and then shrugged. "Sometimes. Depends on how horny I am, how softly he does it."

I nodded, filing that away for later. "Anyway, I laughed because it tickled really bad and pulled his hand away. He tried again and this time he got all the way up my shirt and he was kissing my neck and stuff."

She nodded, wanting to hear more.

"Anyway, so we did it. He took my virginity, and none too nicely either. He just pumped in a few times and then rolled off me and went to the bathroom."

Her feet slowed as she stared at me. "Wait...you guys did it on your first date?"

I chewed the inside of my lip and nodded, avoiding looking at her now. I already felt a bit slutty and she just confirmed that it was indeed rather slutty to let a guy into your pants on the first date.

"Elly! You have to make the guy wait at least three dates before you give him some milk, as that dumb saying goes."

I nodded slowly.

"So what happened after that? Did he come in and say something crude?" she demanded.

I shook my head, staring at the teeth whitening commercial that was silently playing on the TV. "No. I got dressed and left."

I heard the the thud of a weight hitting the floor on the other side of the mirror just before Kent came around the corner. He had a towel around his neck and lots of sweat pouring out of him, his muscle shirt clinging to him. I gasped and my chest squeezed tightly as fear pumped through me and my feet stopped moving.

Oh no, no, no. Did Kent hear what I'd just said?

I heard Stacy moan softly beside me as she, I assumed, took in the sight of my estranged friend. She leaned over and whispered to me, "Forget that pizza guy. You should move on to someone like him."

"Vanilla Sky?" Kent inquired with a raise of his eyebrow. "Really?" The question hung there for a moment before he spoke again. "I pegged you losing it to Princess Bride." He grinned.

I felt tears pricking at my eyes. He'd heard. He'd heard everything and he thought it was a joke. He thought I was a joke. He thought a guy taking my virginity was hilarious. I was so ashamed and embarrassed that I couldn't look at him. I jumped off the machine and ran to the lady's locker room.

I heard Stacy yelling my name just before I sunk onto the teak slotted bench. Almost as soon as I sat down there was a knock at the door and Kent's voice drifted through it.

"Elly. I was just having some fun. Please, come out."

Having fun? My pain was fun for him? We'd seen each other a total of thirty minutes in the past several months and he thought it gave him the liberty to poke fun at me? "Go away!"

I wiped at my burning eyes and stared at my knees. Briefly I wondered where the hell Stacy was. She was supposed to have my back and fend off stupid boys. All of them. Especially right now since I'd just had the worst male experience of my life. Or close to it.

"Either you come out, or I'm coming in," he said from the other side of the door. "You know I was just messing with you."

Messing with me. Hmph. The only one messing with me was that bastard Kyle and he wouldn't be doing it anymore. I wished at that moment that Kyle were the one about to bust through the door so I could kick him squarely in his balls. Didn't his mother teach him any manners?

After a few seconds I heard him counting, "One...Two..."

I stayed right where I was. I didn't think Kent had the balls to come into the girl's locker room. He might see naked bodies or something and that would be too much for his newly lasered eyeballs to handle. I crossed my arms over my chest and waited for him to go away. I could outlast him.

I was surprised by how quickly my pain was turning into anger. The door opened and there was Kent standing in it. "If there's any other women in here, I'm sorry. I have a friend to talk to." He had one hand over his eyes, the fingers were cracked so they weren't completely covered.

"I'm not your friend, not anymore." I turned around so my back was to him. Seriously, where the hell was Stacy?

"Riddle me this. How many times did you sigh when Wesley finally got Princess Buttercup? How many quotes do you know from the movie?"

What the hell was he going on about? I frowned to myself as I tried to ignore him, but of course he kept going.

"Or was it just me who enjoyed it?"

My mouth ached to open and say something smart-alecky but I kept it closed.

I heard Kent sigh from behind me. "I guess maybe I was the one who wanted that for myself." There was a moment of silence before he continued, "I'm happy for you, Elly. I guess I cut a joke because I wasn't the first one you told. You used to tell me everything. "

I stood up and turned around, unable to keep it in any longer.

"That was before you started dating you-know-who and dropped me like a bad habit! But it doesn't matter and don't be fucking happy for me! It was awful and I never want to have sex again!"

Stacy crept into the locker room and cleared her throat softly. It was about damn time!

"You can't swear off sex. It is an amazing thing. You'll like it, eventually, I promise. You just need to do it with the right guy. A guy who deserves you." His hand moved away from his eyes and he turned his head to look at Stacy who waved at him. The traitor. One look from Kent and she was as harmless as a sleeping kitten.

"Jesus. Should I leave you two alone?" I motioned between them.

Stacy's eyes finally looked at me and she shook her head, "No, no! But he's right. You can't swear off sex because of that jerk."

I covered my eyes with my hand and let out a deep sigh. Why was this happening to me? What had I ever done to deserve this?

"Elly. I'm sorry for cracking the joke. I really am, okay?" He sounded sorry but I wasn't going to let him get off that easily. He should've known better than to say something so stupid.

I lowered my hand, the tears were still threatening to spill as I looked at him, his pitiful expression only making me feel worse. "How sorry are you? Sorry enough to let me punch you?"

Stacy gasped. "Elly! Don't punch him!"

He covered his junk with both hands and nodded, "Go ahead. Punch it out." He closed his eyes tightly and his body tensed.

I looked between him and Stacy and sighed softly. "It's not you I want to punch. Not really."

Stacy exhaled in relief as Kent's eyes opened. "So you don't want to hit me now?" His hands slowly moved back to his sides.

As I stared at him the image of who I really wanted to hurt was in my head. Kyle, Kyle who had hurt me and had taken the one thing that I hadn't even really wanted to give to him. I couldn't ever get that back. I couldn't get that moment back. That's what hurt the most.

I pressed my lips together tightly so that I wouldn't sob and shook my head, my eyes dropped as the tears spilled down my cheeks. It felt like an eternity before I felt Kent's strong, warm arms come around me.

"Quit crying. We're gonna go do something fun," he said softly. He swayed slowly with me in his arms.

"Like what?" My voice sounded foreign to my ears, it was thick with tears.

"Can't tell you that, Els. It would ruin the surprise."

Chapter 4

After we'd both showered and I'd said goodbye to Stacy, Kent put me in his crappy car and ran around to join me. I settled back into the passenger seat which used to fit my body like a glove. It sagged a bit now. I buckled up and smiled as he did the same. "Are you going to tell me where we're going now?"

"No. Quit asking or I'll turn this car around."

I scoffed. "I dare you."

He looked over at me with a sly grin on his lips. "You dare me, huh?"

I met his grin with a challenging lift of my eyebrows and an indifferent shrug of my shoulders. "Yep. Turn this car around. See if I care," I said. He turned the car on and carefully backed out of the space as some offending metal band screamed through the speakers. "Oh my god! How can you listen to that?" I covered one ear and put the other to my shoulder to try to block it out as I reached forward with my other hand to turn it off.

He was snickering beside me. "It gets me out of my head for a little while."

"What's wrong with being inside your head?"

"Lots of things. So... it was awful, huh?"

I really didn't want to talk about this. Not with him. He obviously didn't take it seriously. I'd been sober when I'd lost mine, unlike Kent had been, and I would remember every single detail for the rest of my life.

"Yep. It wasn't great, that's for sure."

"Well, if it makes you feel any better it wasn't really good for me until...," he trailed off and then sighed. "Alright, I can't lie to you. It's pretty much always good for me. But I'm a guy. I am pretty sure that it's different for you chicks." His tone was relaxed but his body was tense, he gripped the steering wheel tightly, showing white knuckles. And he kept clenching his jaw, it flickered beneath his skin.

"We don't have to talk about this, you know." I looked out the window. "I'd actually prefer it if we didn't talk about this. It's...weird."

He sighed loudly and he mumbled, "Thank god," under his breath. His body instantly relaxed behind the wheel. I shook my head a little. Same old Kent. Sex and me didn't go together. Ever. Not in his world. That much hadn't changed.

I looked around as we pulled into a parking spot, confusion setting in as to why we were at the liquor store. I looked at him and frowned. "What are we doing here? Neither of us are old enough to get booze."

He put his hand on my shoulder and gave me a look of pity. "Oh, Els. You stay here. You can't go in there, you'd blow my cover." He chuckled as he got out of his car and went into the store. I looked around nervously as I waited for him. What if a cop came and saw me in the car outside the liquor store? What if a robber came by and tried to do the deed while we were here? What if... I didn't get to finish my thought because Kent came back to the car with a large brown paper bag under his arm. He tried to the handle but I'd locked the car. He knocked on the window and then stooped down to look at me. He cocked his head to the side and raised his eyebrows causing me to giggle.

His voice was muffled through the glass, "Come on, Elly. Open the damn door." He stood back up and looked around, waiting for me.

I unlocked the door and then, just before he could open it, I locked it again. He stooped down and frowned. "Elly!"

I grinned some more. I could've done that all night but when I noticed that a cop had pulled up a few spaces down I unlocked the door and hunched down in my seat. Kent got in casually and twisted around to put the bag in the backseat. "Play it cool, Els. You're going to get us caught."

I shook my head, staying low in my seat as the cops got out of their cruiser. My view was blocked when Kent's body came over mine, his head ducking between my neck and shoulder. His breath on my skin tickled and caused me to giggle and push him away. I tried, anyway, but he was too heavy. "Kent!"

"Just pretend I'm making out with you, weirdo."

"Won't that make them stare?"

There was a pause before he pulled away and started the car. "You're right." He tugged on my seatbelt and then pulled out of his parking spot. I wasn't sure where we were going now, but with alcohol involved it was sure to be a good time regardless, right?

We drove for fifteen minutes, through the city, past the suburbs and onto a few winding roads until we stopped in front of a very tall metal structure.

"You are lucky that I know you well to know that you don't want to kill me. Please tell me this isn't where you take Jen on dates."

He laughed as he got out of the car. He came back in, his hands on his seat as he leaned towards me, "No. Jen knows nothing about this secret spot of mine. And you'd better not tell her. It would be a friendship-breaker."

I raised one brow, he was being weirder than usual. "Alright. I don't think you have to worry about that. I'd have to actually talk to her first."

He leaned over more and kissed my forehead quickly before grabbing the bag. I wiped his kiss off my head and then got out of the car too. I took a step back so that I could look all the way to the top of the tower. This could be fun.

Luckily it wasn't too windy and the cold chill of fall had yet to settle. It was a warm night, perfect for being up high where the bugs would leave you alone. "So you've been here before?"

"Yep. And it's completely safe, unless you jump off. I can't guarantee that you'll live if you do that."

"Sounds reasonable."

He chuckled and led the way up the metal ladder. He was a little slow because of the booze he was holding. When we got to the top I took a few minutes to walk around and check it out. I got down onto my belly and pulled myself to the edge to have a look all the way down. Just as my neck was clear of the edge I felt something clamp around my calf.

"Don't jump!"

I screamed and kicked my legs. I heard Kent laughing behind me. He loved scaring me, the jerk. I rolled over and sat up. "That was not funny!"

"Says you. You couldn't see the look on your face."

"And neither will you when I punch you in both your eyes."

He chuckled as he sat down beside me and opened a brown glass bottle with the picture of a peach on it. "So violent today, Els. What happened to the little innocent grunge singer I used to hang out with?"

"She was abandoned by her best friend when he started dating a blonde bimbo." I grabbed the bottle from him and took a swig. It burned and only faintly tasted of peaches. I coughed as I pushed the bottle back to him. He took it and was smiling at me when I could open my eyes to look. "What?" I barked.

"I've missed you. That's all."

The way his eyes stared at me, like he was soaking me up, seeing me for the first time, made me uncomfortable. I nudged him and looked away, "You're not drunk enough to get mushy with me." My heart was beating wildly in my chest. I wanted nothing more than for him to get mushy with me. I wanted Kent, for myself. Part of me was hating him for making me give my v-card to another dude. It should've been him and it should've been years ago, even if I was fatter.

I heard the liquid swish inside the bottle as Kent took a swig. "You know, I was wondering if you'd still had it. I thought maybe you'd lost your virginity a while ago."

I laughed, amused that he would think anyone was interested in fat Elly. He hadn't been, why on Earth would he have expected for someone else to be? "Yeah, no." I sighed softly after I took the bottle from him and took another drink.

"The way you talked about Tony I thought for sure..."

I took another drink. I had made Tony up the summer between high school and college, hoping to make Kent jealous. It hadn't worked. "Nope."

"Huh. Well, it's done with now. And you feel like you're at the bottom, right?" I nodded and he continued, "So there's nowhere left to go but up."

And up we were. I kicked my legs and stared at the blackness underneath them. "Why did you bring me up here?"

"Because when I'm feeling upset this is where I like to go. To put things into perspective. Nothing has ever been so bad that I've wanted to jump, so that's a good thing, I guess." He reached out and tried to take the bottle but I held tight. Our eyes met and I saw in his something sad. Loneliness? Regret? I wasn't sure. He tugged and I tugged back and soon I was on top of him, laughing. And a moment later he stopped laughing and stared at me as I'd seen him stare at me before when we were younger and alone in his room. He looked as if he were going to kiss me. But it never happened in the past and it wasn't going to happen now. And before he could reject me I rolled over and stared at the stars.

I pointed to a group of stars, "Look, it's Kyle's penis."

"There?" He motioned with his finger to a large cluster of stars.

"No," I said. "There." I motioned, outlining something very small.

Chapter 5

I walked into the Art History class on the first day of the new semester and found a pleasant surprise sitting in the back of the lecture hall with his notebook out and his pencil writing furiously. Kent.

He didn't notice me as I slowly approached him, like a cat stalking its prey. I grinned as I sat down beside him, whispering as I pulled out my pen and flipped my notebook open, "I heard this professor is a real hard ass..."

Kent looked up from his notes towards my familiar voice. "Wait... you have this class too?" He looked around as if he was going to be punk'd or something. A small smile formed on his lips as his eyes settled on me.

"Yeah...gotta get that art credit somehow. And you know me, I'm no artist when it comes to my hands." I smacked my forehead and shook my head. "That...came out wrong."

A little blush touched Kent's cheeks as he laughed. "Oh, Elly. Still the slip of the lips, I see. I'm excited to have some time carved out three times a week to talk to you."

The professor walked in and the lights went down. I looked at Kent in the darkness, the only light shining on his face was from the slides the professor projected onto the front wall of the classroom. I wondered what he would do if I touched his knee. Or blew in his ear. I was still slightly sore from my disaster of a date but it was quickly sliding away the longer I stared at him. His new and improved biceps were going to be my newest obsession. They bulged delightfully with each movement of his hand. He'd always been cute to me, but damn, he was turning into the quite the man.

I forced myself to focus on the lecture and write down some notes. I was doing very well in college and I wasn't about to fudge that up now. My mother would kill me.

Halfway through class I cleared my throat and whispered to Kent, "You were saying about the talking part?"

Kent chuckled softly and whispered back, his breath on my neck giving me goosebumps and hard nipples. "I was saying that I'm really looking forward to talking with you after class."

The professor stopped in the middle of his discussion about surrealism and Salvador Dali. "I see I'm boring a few of my students. Mr...?"

Kent turned his face away from me and I felt a loss and a squeeze in my chest. The professor was staring at Kent with an eyebrow raised, the slide projector remote pressed against his rounded belly.

"Lytle... sir..."

The professor grimaced, clearly annoyed. "Would you like to talk about Salvador Dali since you seem to be interested in speaking during my lecture?"

Kent ran his hand through his hair. Oh god, what had I done? Was he going to flunk art history class because of me? I was about to confess my guilt when Kent started to speak.

"He was born in 1904 in Spain, died in 1989. He's the father of surrealism in today's standards of art. His most elaborate work was titled 'The Persistence of Memory' crafted in 1931."

Some of the other students mumbled to each other, awed by the balls he had to make the professor look like a dick. And impressed that he knew his shit.

The professor didn't look happy, his humiliation tactic had failed and blown up in his face. "Mr. Lytle. I'd like to see you after class, please." As the professor continued on with his lecture Kent looked at me and winked.

I couldn't help but giggle. Good thing Kent did some studying before class. Had the professor called on me I'd have been embarrassed just as he would've wanted. And I never would've said another peep in his class again.

I scribbled notes in my notebook and five minutes before the end of class I realized my leg was pressed against Kent's. I sat up, pulled my leg away, and immediately missed the warmth he'd provided. I continued to write notes, nibbling on the end of my pen when it wasn't something I felt I needed to write down.

The lights went up signaling the end of class. Kent rustled his things to get it in the bag. "You asleep yet?" he asked as he stood with me. "Oh, and since I haven't had the chance to tell you, you look awesome, Elly. I mean it. I'm proud of all your hard work." Kent put his arm over my shoulder.

"Mr. Lytle. My office, please." The professor killed our mini-moment.

I tried not to make a big deal of it, but I couldn't stop the tingles coursing through my body despite the fact that it had been an innocent, platonic touch. He still made my heart rate go through the roof and my loins sizzle. "Oooooh. You're in trouble." I teased, slapping him playfully on his arm.

"Well, if someone wasn't trying to talk to me, maybe I wouldn't have had to be a smart ass."

"Like it's my fault you're a smart ass," I scoffed.

He was still grinning as he started down the stairs towards the exit. "You want to grab a tea and hang out outside? If the professor doesn't murder me, that is."

"Um...maybe some other time. I've got an audition to get to." I smiled softly and gathered up my notebook.

Truthfully, I didn't want to catch Jen's shit if she saw us outside having coffee together without her. I wondered if Kent was going to tell Jen that we had a class together...in the dark. And I'd love to be a fly on the wall if and when he did tell her.

"Alright, well," he stood there awkwardly for a moment, "good luck with the audition then. If I don't see you later then I guess it'll be Wednesday in here." Kent smiled at me over his shoulder as he slipped out the door.

I watched him leave and immediately felt the loss. I exhaled loudly and stared at the ceiling for a moment as I collected my nerves. I looked up to the seats at the top of the lecture hall as I was leaving and didn't see the incoming guy. We collided with full body contact and fell backwards, our things falling between us. "Ooh, I'm sorry!" I was blushing as I gathered up my notebook.

The guy was smiling, a dimple in his chin like Kent had. But this guy was blonde and a little taller and he had blue eyes. He was staring at me as he blocked the doorway. I smiled nervously and hugged my notebook to my chest. "Are you going to let me through? I have to get to another class."

"I do too. But I think you should pay a fine for almost killing us both by not looking where you were going." His hands slipped into the front pockets of his jeans and my eyes followed. My knees almost gave out when his thick southern accent coated his words.

I swallowed hard as the outline of his penis pushed against the front of his pants. I pulled my gaze to his face, sure that my face was beet red from blushing. Suddenly I wasn't a virgin anymore and I was checking out every guy's junk? "Oh? And, um...What do you want? To bully money out of me?"

"No, no, darlin'. I just wanna take you out to dinner."

"I can't." I looked down further, taking note of his cowboy boots.

"Why not?"

"I don't date men who listen to country music. It's against my values." His laughter vibrated through me and I clutched my notebook tighter, sure that I was going to faint if he kept hitting on me. He was hot, like really hot.

"Imagine my luck. I stopped listening to it this morning. Went cold turkey."

"Sounds like you'll be in a sour mood then and not good company for dinner," I said.

He laughed again and I nearly melted. "You're really gonna make a cowboy beg?" He kept his hands on the doorway and leaned forward, speaking lowly into my ear. The hot breath accompanying his words sent tingles between my thighs. "I'll do it, pretty girl. Please don't embarrass us further. It's just dinner."

"Okay, fine." I stepped back and tried to act as if I weren't affected. "I'll meet you a Mexicali at nine tonight. Don't be late."

He winked at me and then made his way past me, purposely brushing his arm against my chest as he passed, heading for an empty seat. I felt his eyes on me as I left the lecture hall and I couldn't shake the smile he'd put on my face.

Chapter 6

Mexicali was terrific and it paved the way for several more dates with Mr. Will, the cowboy. I waited for him after every Art History class just so I could make out with him for a few brief minutes before he had to disappear into the lecture hall for his PoliSci class. The chemical touches from Kent only warmed me up for the giant sparks that flew between Will and I.

I made sure he bought me at least three dinners before hopping in the sack with him. Three weeks passed and as suddenly as it'd started he'd stopped calling. He made out with me before class Monday, Wednesday, and Friday, but blew me off when I tried to make plans with him in the evenings.

I figured he was just losing interest so I did what any girl would do... I asked my male friend for advice.

"Kent, I don't get it. What am I doing wrong? Will and I we were close, you know? And suddenly he just...stopped." I studied Kent's face, noted that his jaw was clenched tightly.

"Elly, I love you, you know that but, I really don't want to talk about this stuff with you."

I frowned and pouted. "Would you rather I talk to some other guy about it? How embarrassing would that be? Come on, Kent. I'm asking for your advice, as a dude. I value your opinion."

He sighed and gripped the hair on the top of his head for a brief second before pounding the desk with his open palms. "Fine.

If you want my opinion he's probably found another girl. College guys are notorious for being players."

I felt my face fall and looked away.

"So you don't think a college guy could fall in hopelessly in love with me and end up asking me to marry him?"

"I didn't say that, Els. I said this particular guy isn't really sounding like he's very interested."

I nodded and turned my body away from Kent's. Maybe he was the wrong person to ask. He was, after all, a guy who fell hard for the first girl who showed any interest in him at all. Well, for the first pretty, rich girl who had. I had shown interest way before that, but he'd ignored me.

"Well, let's say for the sake of the argument that he was interested in me, or at least that I wanted to try to surprise him with something special. Do you have any ideas or...?" I felt Kent's eyes on me but I didn't dare look up to meet his gaze. It was embarrassing enough without him seeing the desperation in my eyes.

"I'm probably not the best guy to ask. I'd be happy enough just to have you at all. I wouldn't need anything extra." My head whipped towards him and he shook his head, putting his hands up defensively, "I mean, if I was into you. If you were more than a friend, you know."

I nodded and looked away, my hopeful heart deflated once again. Yeah, that sounded about right.

"Great. Well, thanks for nothing," I said.

He groaned softly, "What do you want me to say, Elly? Show up at his door wearing sexy lingerie?"

I thought about that for a moment before turning in my seat, a large smile on my lips. "You're a genius!" I was still smiling when the lights went down and the professor started the day's lecture.

* * *

I tightened the tie at the waist of the ankle-length coat I wore and exhaled slowly, trying to get the courage to knock on Will's door. I could hear his TV playing on the other side of the door but not much else. He was probably studying. I turned to leave, I could just talk to him later.

I shook my head and turned back around. I was here and in the new black lace teddy I'd bought between classes earlier. I lifted my hand and knocked loudly on his door. I waited a beat and the tried for the knob. It was unlocked so I went inside, maybe he was in the bathroom and I could surprise him with me on his bed.

My eyes darted around the room and landed on the moving lumps under Will's comforter. Will's head popped out and I caught a glimpse of blonde hair beneath him. I cinched my waistband tighter, the blood leaving my face.

"God, I guess we really are over."

"Elly, baby. This ain't what it looks like."

I laughed and held my hands up, shaking my head. "I'm not an idiot. I'll leave you two to your...philandering," I said loudly.

Will didn't bother to get out of bed, he just lay there, protecting the girl from my view. Maybe he'd cheated on me with her. Maybe that's why he was trying so hard to keep her from seeing me.

As I left I felt the sting of yet another rejection. What the hell was wrong with me? Or was it just the boys that I picked. I needed comfort and despite what my head was telling me I knew in my heart that I needed Kent.

* * *

I found myself at Kent's dorm. I knocked on the door and looked around as I waited for an answer, my mascara had been running, and I'm sure I looked every bit as messy as I felt on the inside.

The door opened and there was Kent wearing a tank top and a pair of shorts. When he saw me a smile started to form, but it soon faded when he saw the condition I was in. "Elly, what's wrong?"

"I..." I crossed my arms over my chest and tried to look behind him into the dorm. Despite how much I wanted him to hold me I didn't want to have Jen's hatred pointed at me and I didn't want his roommates to be seeing me in this state either. "Is Jen here? Or your roommates?" My voice was wavering and I was fighting back more tears.

Kent shook his head slowly. "No, she went out a while ago.

Said she had to meet her parents. And my roommates are at the game."

His hand came out and grasped one of mine, sending slow sizzles up my arm. I pushed it down, tried to ignore it. "Come in here, Elly. It's all right." He pulled me inside even though I hesitated. Once inside he shut the door and lead me to his bed. "Sit down. I'll get you some water."

I sat down on his bed and wiped at my eyes, smearing the mascara sideways on my cheeks. I rubbed my fingers on the trench coat nervously. I stayed quiet, afraid that once I said something the tears would come bursting out right along with the words.

Kent came back with a bottle of water in his hand, which he offered to me. I took the bottle as he sat down next to me. "Elly. You can tell me what happened if you want. I'll listen." Kent's hand reached out and came to rest on my knee. I ignored those little sparks too. And tried to ignore the fact that I was wearing nothing but trashy lingerie under the coat.

I took unscrewed the cap and took a tiny sip of water, my eyes on the plastic as it came down to rest on my other knee. My voice was soft, a whisper as I voiced my internal thoughts aloud, "What is so wrong with me? Why can't I be enough?" I sniffled and wiped at my nose with the back of my hand, still not looking at him. I pretended he wasn't there. I didn't want to see the pity in his eyes for his old friend, but if anyone knew the answer it had to be him.

I felt his hand cup my chin and let him lift my face, my eyes slowly meeting his gaze. I was surprised that I didn't see pity there, but rather something warmer, friendlier. "Elly. You're amazing," he said softly and his thumb rubbed a trail of a tear from my cheek. "Fuck that guy. He just didn't know what he had."

I pulled my chin away from his grasp and laughed humorlessly, looking away from his gaze. It was a trick. Another trick, another lie. "Fucking that guy was the mistake. Now he's fucking some blonde whore. Am I... Am I just expecting too much from college boys? Maybe...maybe I shouldn't even be upset...Maybe it's just natural to fuck a girl one day and then fuck another girl the next day. It was stupid to think that I was special, that a guy could instantly fall in love with me now that I'm thin." I gripped the plastic tighter, and it crumpled slightly in my grasp.

"You can't expect much. Most of them just want to get their rocks off with who ever will let them. Most aren't looking for a solid relationship and the ones who are tend to be tied down." Kent paused and I looked up enough to see that he seemed to be struggling with something but I couldn't tell what it was. "Elly, you know I...I-," his words were cut off by the sound of a knock on the door. He sighed as he got up and answered the door.

I looked at the doorway, Jen was there and looked confused, untrusting as her eyes found me on Kent's bed. "What the hell is going on in here? Is she crying?"

"She is going through some boy trouble."

"Right, and so she came to cry on your shoulder? Hope that you'd feel bad for her and cop a feel?"

I wasn't sure where all that was coming from. And I wasn't sure I wanted to be in the middle of it.

"No, it's not like that, Jen. Come on, you should know that by now." Kent tried to block Jen as she tried to push past him to get to me.

"I'm sorry, this was a mistake," I whispered as I stood up. I should've known that by now too. It wasn't safe to be with Kent. He wasn't that guy anymore. Despite what we'd had in the past he wasn't the one I should be running to with my problems.

Jen scoffed as she got around Kent. She looked at me and then poked Kent in his chest. "I know you wish it were like that. Especially now that she has a hot little body. Don't think I haven't noticed you checking her out. Don't think I haven't noticed you being snippier than usual with me after you ran into her at the party."

Kent left Jen standing there and came back, pushing me back onto his bed. He looked down at me as he said with a frown, "No. You stay. You need someone to talk to, maybe a girl. I need to walk and clear my head. Maybe you two can bitch about how shitty the male population is." Kent turned on his heel and rushed to the door, slamming it behind him as he left the dorm.

I looked at Jen who exhaled slowly and shook her head. "I'm sorry, Elly. I don't mean to drag you in the middle of our shit. It's been hard lately. He just drives me nuts most days...but you don't need to hear it. Did you get a look at that bimbo that boy of yours was fucking?"

Ever since Jen turned eighteen she felt like she could and should use any dirty word that she could think of. On Kent's eighteenth birthday she yelled, "Happy Fucking Birthday, Pussylicker!" in front of his few close friends and his mother. And mine. She was a little inebriated at the time, but it wasn't really a good excuse. I think she lost brownie points with his mom for that. I certainly would have if I had said it.

I shook my head. "Not really, just saw some blonde hair..."

Jen just shook her head and took a seat next to me. "What a bitch. I can't believe some women." Jen was quiet for a moment before she spoke again. "Elly, thank you for being my friend." Jen put her arms around my shoulders.

I gave her a polite hug in return but my mind was churning. I hated these false moments with her. She hated me, clearly, and I didn't like her very much either. I pulled away and then chuckled, "God, I probably look a hot mess. I'm gonna go." I stood up and left Jen sitting there, waiting for Kent who ran into me in the downstairs lobby.

"Elly, hey. Sorry about that. I just...had to get out of there."

He still looked kind of pissed and I was glad he wasn't pissed at me. At least I hoped he wasn't. Maybe I'd interrupted a romantic evening with him and Jen. No, he'd said she was out with her mom.

"It's okay. It was pretty tense in there. Your dorm room is way too small."

He chuckled and it made my belly feel warm.

"Yeah, tell me about it."

"No time for cru—" Oh no, maybe I'd interrupted his private boy time. "Oh god, did I come stop by at the worst time? I'm sure you don't get alone time very often and—"

He stopped me with his hand as he placed it on my shoulder. "Elly. Stop. You didn't interrupt anything. I was playing a video game, that's all. I'm sorry I can't keep talking about how awesome you are."

I rolled my eyes, totally not believing him. "Whatever." I nodded and smiled, not feeling it in my heart but I needed to show it for his sake. "Better go up there and patch things up with your girlfriend."

"Yeah, I'd better or she won't play with me." I blinked at him and he shook his head, stuttering with embarrassment, "N-no! I m-meant video games!"

I nodded a couple of times slowly. "Right. Okay. Not my business." I held my hands up innocently and side stepped around him.

He raked his fingers through his hair as he watched me go. "Elly! That's not what I meant!"

"Go on. Go play with your girlfriend." I shuddered as I walked out of his dorm. I didn't want that image in my head. I closed my eyes as I walked a few steps. Rainbows. The beach. Crabs. CRABS! I opened my eyes and shook my head. I needed to go work out and sap the self-pity from my body.

Chapter 7

I sat down next to Kent a few days later in Art History class. "Hey." I opened my notebook and uncapped my pen.

Kent didn't look like himself. It looked like he hasn't slept well in days. He had his notebook out like always, but he didn't have his pencil in hand. He turned his eyes towards me and offered a little smile. "Hey, Elly."

I looked him over and bent over slightly so I could get a better look at him. The bags under his eyes were huge. "What-are you okay?"

Kent rubbed his eyes and looked back at his notebook. "Yeah, just not been sleeping well is all."

"Oh, right," I sat back in my seat and stared down at my notebook. "Too many late nights with Jen lately, huh?"

Kent shook his head and picked up his pencil. He started doodling on the cover of his notebook. That was one of his pissed off tells. "No. I've been sleeping on her couch."

"And why is that?" I glanced between his face and his doodles. "I thought you and Jen made up."

The professor turned down the lights which signified he was ready to speak.

I wrote a note on his clean page as he opened his notebook.

I can get that coffee after class today.

When Kent started taking notes I did as well, the professor wasted no time getting down to business. At class's end I stood up, notebook in hand. "So do you have time?"

Kent stood up he nodded his head. "I thought you'd never ask."

I smiled and walked with him down the stairs. "Why don't you break up with her?"

"It's not that easy. Sometimes she doesn't take no for an answer. There are sometimes she's really sweet, but as of late it's like she's a totally different person."

I chewed on my lower lip softly. "But you love her, right?"

"That's a very complicated question, Elly. One I'm not sure I even know the answer to. Ever since prom night I thought so. I mean she didn't just leave me there after I passed out. She said we had sex, but I can't really remember."

"No, she did...I, um...I walked in on you guys. It was the worst night of my life." I avoided his gaze as the night replayed in my memory.

That night I had tried to be a good sport, for Kent's sake, but prom blew big chunks. The only person I'd wanted to dance with had abandoned me. Come to prom with us, Elly, he'd said. It'll be fun, he'd said. He had lied. It hadn't been fun. It hadn't been fun at all.

I started my walk to the hotel lobby when I saw a group of guys crowded around a half open door. Curiosity got the better of me and I pushed my way to the front, ready to close the door on whatever the jerks were staring at. But that was before I saw Jen, her short mini-dress pushed all the way up, revealing her whole perfect naked body. The guys were staring at it, soaking up the memory for the spank bank. And I couldn't look away. I should have but I couldn't. I saw Kent, on the floor of the Pine Room, his hands on Jen's waist as she bounced on top of his half naked body.

I didn't stay to see more than thirty seconds before I ran off. I could faintly hear their comments and their laughter. "Aww, poor Elly-phant."

His voice was soft, bringing me back to the present, "I'm sorry you had to see that, Elly."

"I am too, but you can't take back the past." I shook my head to try to get rid of the memory. It only ever worked temporarily.

Kent shook his head as they came to the little coffee shop on campus. "You going to let me buy your coffee?" He no doubt switched the subject since we were getting close to other people.

"Um, no." I looked down at my feet. "Sorry, sorry I brought that up. I forget that I can't talk to you about everything."

He shook his head. "I just don't remember it at all. It's one of those things that I wished I could remember. Your first time is supposed to be special. At least memorable. Jen never told me exact details. Pretty much like now, she only tells me half of the things she's doing. Sometimes it just doesn't seem to add up or something." It seemed Kent was opening up a little more, getting more comfortable with himself. I was glad to see it. It was a nice change from his self-conscious high school self.

"I..." I shook my head, wondering if I should tell him anything at all about my social life. Of course I should. He's my friend. I sighed, feeling stupid for even thinking of keeping him isolated from the rest of my life. "So, I'm uh...I'm singing at open mic night tomorrow. I figured I'd invite you and Jen to come see me. You know, if you want to." I shrugged softly as I stepped up to the coffee counter and ordered my chai tea. I paid in cash and then stepped aside so Kent could order. I figured changing the subject would be easier than telling my friend that he needed to get his head out of his ass and pay attention to his feelings. I wasn't very good at it either so I couldn't really fault him.

Kent nodded his head. "I'd like that. I'm sure I can convince Jen to go."

I doubted it very much but I nodded politely anyway. "Good luck with that." I poked his side with my free hand. I shook my finger and winced, "Ouch. You're like a rock these days."

Kent chuckled as he ordered his drink. He lifted up his shirt to show his abs. "Not bad for a dorky kid, huh?" He let the shirt drop. His drink came up and he took it in hand.

I tried not to stare so I looked around instead. "Oh god, Kent. You're drawing the wolves' attention. They're going to come maul you if you do that again." I grinned. "I'd show you my abs but then you'd just be super emasculated."

Kent laughed as he put his arm around my shoulder and walked us to a table. I didn't embrace him back but just walked casually as if it were no big thing that my high school crush turned super hottie had his arm around me. And that he smelled like a nighttime forest. And that I wanted to smack the coffee out of his hand and have my way with him on every table in the joint. "You laugh, but that's only because you haven't seen them. And you probably never will. I don't like seeing grown men cry," I said.

"Right, right. Maybe we'll have to go to the gym sometime and see who's better at what. Or maybe just work out together. Mike would love it if you'd join in. He'd get to stare at you. It would be a nice change. It's pretty creepy when he stares at me." He led us to a table where he took a seat.

I sat down across from him and chuckled, "I'm sure you'd have no trouble finding a girl to work out with you two. There are lots of PYT's dying for attention from two strapping college men like yourselves."

Kent shook his head. "I don't want to do that. It's enough dealing with Jen when I have a hot friend, much less more girls trying to force their way in."

"Woah, woah...back up." I motioned backwards with my hand, "You think I'm hot?" I raised my eyebrows to match the surprise I felt.

"Yes. Why are you surprised? You were cute before, but you're smoking now. So, does it feel good to hear that from guys? See the way they look at you?" Kent took a drink of his iced coffee.

I shrugged, "Guys actually approach me now, but I wouldn't say anyone looks at me differently." Not that I paid much attention. "And yes, I am surprised to hear you admit that you find me attractive. It only took what...?" I looked up and pretended to mentally count. "Like ten years?"

Kent scoffed and shook his head. "You wanted to hear me say it for that long?" He smiled.

I smiled back. "Longer, probably. That's okay, though, I'm on my way to out-sexing you. I'm going to leave your monogamous ass in the dust." I sipped my tea, trying hard to make light of my guy situation.

That playful smile wavered for a moment but whatever he'd been thinking had quickly passed. "Yeah, yeah. If you count how much I've had then you've still got a way to go, Elly." He stuck his tongue out at me just as his phone played a few notes.

I kicked his shin under the table. "Oops." And then looked away innocently.

Kent grabbed at his shin under the table as he made a pained face and pulled the phone from his pocket. When he looked at it he sighed. "It's Jen. She's wondering where I am."

"Okay, well, I guess you should get going."

He pushed the ignore button and stuffed it back into his pocket. "Nah. She can wait. I'm with my friend right now." I was about to burst on the inside. Had he really just ignored Jen for me? It was like a dream come true! I tried my best to keep my smiles on the inside.

"You are talking about me, right?" I asked. He was leaned back, his body language exuding how comfortable he was around me. And his deep chocolate eyes stared at me, they seemed to sparkle more now that they weren't hidden behind his glasses.

He smirked. "Who else would I be talking about?"

"Not who. What." My eyes dropped to his crotch which was just barely visible beneath the table. Was there a bulge there? My eyes darted back up and caught sight of a little color on his cheeks.

"No, you pervert. Were you just checking out my junk?"

"What? I," I scoffed, "no. Why would I? Ew." I shook my head in mock disgust and watched as he failed to believe me. "Apparently all the working out you've been doing has been going to your head. Your ego is a little too big if you think I'd be checking out your junk." Apparently that had hit something because he dropped his gaze to his cup.

"You're right. I have become somewhat of a jerk." He looked so defeated that I just wanted to hug him and take it back. Just as I was about to apologize he stood up. "Come on, Elly."

I shook my head as I looked up at him, "Where are we going?"

"Someplace where it's hard to be a jerk."

Where the hell would that be? I stood up, finished the last of the coffee and threw my cup into the trash as we exited. We walked through campus until we reached his car. I had a lot of questions but now wasn't the time to be asking them in case it ruined whatever new scheme he had in his brain.

He turned the radio to my favorite station and sang along loudly with me when the latest Mariah Carey song came on. I had no idea he still listened to pop music. If he did, it was probably Jen's doing and thinking about Jen was going to ruin my happy mood so I pushed the thought aside and pretended, while I could, that Jen didn't exist.

Kent joined a little line of cars waiting to park in a large, dusty parking lot that was only used a handful of times every year. This time of the year was County Fair time. I hadn't been to the fair since freshman year in high school. Last time I'd come it had also been with Kent. It was the first time our mothers let us go anywhere alone without adult supervision. I, being naive as I was, had fantasies of my best friend kissing me on the ferris wheel and romantically feeding me funnel cake. Instead we walked around, played games, pet some farm animals and joined a pie eating contest, of which Kent won.

I was smiling as Kent lifted his hips to withdraw his wallet from his back pocket to pay for parking. "Excited, Els?"

"Hells yes! I haven't been here since—"

He interrupted me. "Freshman year." His grin was contagious.

"Yes," I confirmed.

After we parked the car we got out and headed into the fair, which wasn't too crowded because it was so early in the day. We went to the farm animals first.

"I never understood why you liked this part. They stink," he said.

I bent down next to a pen that held a couple of lambs and smiled as their little heads popped out. "Because they're trapped here. And they're beautiful, despite the smell they omit." I grabbed some hay from their feeding box and held it out as they came over to eat it. I heard the electronic shutter noise and looked up. Kent was smiling, having just taken a picture of me. "What do you think you're doing?"

"Collecting some memories. Duh."

I turned back to the sheep, for some reason that made me sad. Did he think we weren't ever going to come here again? Because of Jen? Because of life in general? Was this just another short little sliver of heaven that I'd have to hold onto forever?

I gave each of the lambs a pet and then stood up. I forced a smile as I pulled out my phone and snapped a picture of Kent who was bent over the pig pen, his lips puckered as he made kissing noises to try to get its attention. "Perfect. Give her a little kiss for the camera." I was able to admire my photo for only a second before Kent was coming towards me.

"Is it bad? Let me see."

"Oh no, it's great." I backed away quickly and stuffed my camera into my book bag.

"Elly, let me see!"

I shook my head and ran away. He gave chase until I stopped at the funnel cake booth. I inhaled deeply and then moaned. The smell of sweet fried dough was so deliciously sinful. I inhaled one more time, my eyes closed.

"Just buy one, already." Kent's voice was at my side.

I looked at him and shook my head. "Are you nuts?"

"Probably." He grinned as he approached the booth. He came back a minute later with a steaming plate of funnel cake, lots of napkins and one fork. He held it under my nose. I inhaled and moaned again. He brought it over to a little table and sat down. I sat down next to him on the bench and looked around, trying ignore the temptation. A few seconds later Kent was moaning. I looked and was about to say something when a forkful of funnel cake entered my mouth.

It was just the right temperature and heavenly. I chewed it slowly, savoring it as it seemed to melt on my tongue. "Oh god." When I came out of my funnel cake orgasm I looked up and noted a blush on Kent's cheeks. "What's wrong?"

"I just...forgot how, um, passionate you were about food," he said.

It was my turn to blush. "Sorry."

"Hey, it's fine. I just wish I'd thought to put a hat out to collect tips." He chuckled and I smacked his arm.

"Who is the perv now?"

He laughed. "That guy that walked by and ducked down to see if anything was going on in your pants."

"Ew." I shuddered, chuckling along with him.

After we finished the funnel cake, I'm pretty sure I only ate half, we walked around for a bit. It was so nice to just be with him. And have his full attention. And feel like I used to, before Jen. I felt confident, beautiful, and it was all because of him and the way he was with me, like I was the only one that mattered. The way he'd lightly brush against me and send shivers through my body had me thinking more unsavory thoughts.

We were there for hours, catching up, exchanging jokes, reliving the past. We only had one more thing to do. The ferris wheel. We paid our tickets and got into the metal box. Once we were fastened in they moved us up a notch so they could load the next cart. The sun was going down and it was beautiful. I shivered when we were almost to the top, it was slightly colder fifty feet in the air without trees to break up the wind.

Kent must have noticed because he chuckled and wrapped his arm around my shoulder, pulling me against his warm side. I peeked up at his face and he smiled down at me. "If you're cold you just have to tell me."

"I didn't want to bother you. Or get you in trouble."

His eyes searched mine and he was about to speak when the ride started to move into full rotations. As we went around I looked out at the skyline. Luckily the sun was to our backs so we could see the earth draped in sherbet pink and orange.

"It's beautiful up here," I said softly.

"Yeah." I felt Kent's eyes on me so I looked up. He was looking down at me. That old look in his eyes, the look that always made me think he was about to kiss me. We stared at each other for a long moment but it was broken by the jerking of the ride coming to a stop. Our ride was over, the magic broken. I laughed nervously and tried to sit up and pull away but Kent held onto my shoulder. "Elly..." I waited for him to finish but he never did. He let me go and put his hands on his knees. "Damn. I should've snapped a picture up there."

"There's always next time," I murmured as I straightened up and looked down. Only two more carts before we unloaded. Suddenly I couldn't wait. The reminiscing had only led to yet another let down. Kent wasn't in love with me. He didn't feel for me that way, no matter what his stupid deceiving eyes said. I was a fool for thinking that just because my outsides had improved that he was going to fall all over me. He wasn't interested.

On the way back to campus I turned the station to rock and let it mellow us out. Kent stopped in front of my dorm and put the car into park. I'd been dreading this moment. I hadn't wanted today to end.

I smiled as I unbuckled. "Thanks for today. It was fun."

"Sure. I'll see you in class on Monday."

I nodded and got out of the car. "Bye, Kent."

After I'd made it inside the dorm I saw his car pull away. I spent the rest of the night dreaming about what should've happened on the ferris wheel.

Chapter 8

I looked around the crowded coffee shop nervously. I was about to break my public singing cherry and I wished like hell that I had someone here to support me. I had invited a few people who I knew wouldn't make fun of me but none of them had shown up. I was hoping that Kent would show up, with or without Jen but so far I hadn't seen him either. And I had a feeling in my gut that he wasn't going to show.

Before I knew it my name was announced. I figured it was a waste of time but I looked around one more time before stepping up onto the stage. I was looking for a tall, dark haired man. The same tall, dark-haired man who I'd grown up with. I was even looking for his tall blonde companion but I didn't see either of them in the sea of faces.

I exhaled slowly and then smiled as I sat down. My fingers plucked nervously on the guitar as I strummed it. Adrenaline took over as I started my set and before I knew it, it was over and the crowd was applauding enthusiastically.

I was so proud and relieved as I stepped off the stage. My first performance had gone great. No one had snickered or booed. What more could an amateur musician ask for?

As I stepped down off stage I sat back down to listen to the other acts of the evening, letting the adrenaline slowly leave my body.

The MC announced Nate and I felt my breath catch in my

throat as this dark haired Adonis stepped onto the stage. His speaking voice had a soft quality to it, but his singing voice was incredible. I couldn't take my eyes off him, his stage presence was amazing. He sang about love and loss and admiration.

I watched as he walked off the small stage and disappeared into the crowd. I turned back to the stage and sat for another twenty minutes before rising to leave. I had to get up early for class. I stood up and grabbed my guitar and headed towards the exit.

Just before I reached it, I stumbled into someone's guitar. "Woah! Sorry." I reached for the guitar laying on the floor at the same time as its owner. Nate. My heart stuttered but somehow I managed enough courage to speak, softly because people were still performing, "Hey, you were great up there."

He stood up, his hands still holding onto the guitar. I released it, and hoped he didn't think I was trying to run away with it. "Thanks. You were great too. You have a beautiful voice."

I blushed and pushed some of my hair behind my ear. When I glanced up his dark eyes were still looking at me. He was taller than I realized and I had to tilt my head back as he stepped outside with me.

"Want to grab a coffee or something?" he asked. My eyes searched his, a small smile played on his lips, his face was darkened from the scruff of a day old shave.

"We just left a coffeehouse..."

His lips turned up into a grin as he glanced away briefly and then looked back at me. "You're right. I had three cups of coffee too." He chuckled softly and tugged on his left ear, drawing my attention to it. I wanted to nibble on it and whisper into it. "Well, how about we go get dessert somewhere then?"

I looked back at his face, which was flawless except for a tiny scar above his right eyebrow. I nodded. "Sure." I looked around trying to gather my sense of direction. "Um, there is a diner down that way," I pointed to the left, "or a bakery a couple blocks that way." I pointed to the right and watched as his head turned in both direction as he considered the options.

"A bakery sounds less skeezy," he said.

I nodded my agreement. I'd probably agree to anything he said. He was gorgeous and my disappointed heart would take whatever he would give me.

"It'll sound more romantic when we tell our grandkids," he said.

I laughed softly, trying to calm my foolish heart, which thought that Nate might be the one. "Wow. We're having grandkids together already?"

"A guy can dream." He winked at me and then turned around, guitar still in hand, and nodded in the direction of the bakery. "Come on, I really want a cupcake now and if the bakery closes before we get there I might just cry."

* * *

It had been a month or so of dating Nate and there were no hiccups in sight. We spent our time together singing and playing guitar. We attended open mic nights together, and we made out a lot. I explained my past relationships, if you could call them that, and he knew I was nowhere near ready to jump on his saddle and ride. He said he respected that and that we could go as slow as I wanted.

After months of retelling my dates to Kent, I realized it was time for them to meet. I wanted to know if Kent's gut feeling about Nate was the same as mine. I wanted approval from my best friend and the only way to get it was for them to spend time together. Kent hadn't liked Will the Cowboy and he had been spot on about him.

I arranged for them to meet us at the bowling alley. It wasn't really Jen's taste, but I had to remind her that I was on a very tight budget. Nate and I were already seated next to each other on the plastic chairs facing the lanes, our dorky shoes on when Kent and Jen walked in. Nate's chocolate brown eyes were accentuated by the maroon and black plaid button down shirt he was wearing.

Tonight was cosmic bowl. Crazy black lights, cheap beers, and ultra loud pop music surrounded us as we sat together, reserving our lane.

"Oh, there they are!"

I waved to get Jen's attention and watched as she approached us. Kent let his eyes move around the bowling alley slowly, I knew he was uncomfortable in loud, crowded public places but he'd just have to get over it.

I stood up and moved to greet them. "Hey! You guys made it!" I had to yell because the music was so loud. Nate came over too and held out his hand, first to Jen then to Nate.

"This is Nate!" I held onto his elbow, an unconscious warning to Jen but when I realized what I was doing I quickly let him go.

"Hey!" He said to both of them in turn. Kent stood there beside Jen with a smile and shook Nate's hand, pumping it a couple of times. I watched as both men sized each other up.

"Can I get us a pitcher of beer or something to eat?" Nate asked.

Kent shook his head towards Nate in response to the question. "I'm good, but Jen might want something to drink."

Jen nodded her head. "A pitcher and some nachos."

Kent made a face and shook his head.

I bit back my grin. "And some waters for me and Kent?" I motioned between us and smiled when Kent winked at me.

Nate nodded. "Sure thing! You guys go get your shoes and get ready for a bowling ass-kicking!" He grinned, and headed towards the bar to order.

Jen couldn't seem to get the grin off her lips as she watched Nate walk away. My fists clenched at my sides.

"Your shoes are waiting!" I forced a smile and pushed them towards the shoe counter. I watched them walk away and blew out a slow breath as I sat down. I was being a little paranoid. Jen was here with Kent. And they were both here to reassure me that my feelings towards Nate were valid. That was it.

They eventually came back and switched out their shoes. I was sitting at the computer, in the process of typing in our names. It was alphabetical so I was up first.

Nate came back with a plate full of nachos slathered with highly processed plastic cheese and a pitcher of beer. The girl behind the counter followed him out with the waters and extra cups for the beer and set them on the table.

Nate smiled at the food and then came up behind me and smacked me on the butt. "Good luck."

I jumped with a grin. "I don't need it!"

I grabbed my hot pink ball and took my first turn. A strike. I whooped and then cabbage patched my way back to my friends, sitting down across from Nate. "Jen! You're up!" Nate and Kent laughed at my antics.

Jen had antics of her own. She had just taken a nacho and put it in her mouth. She licked the cheese from one of her fingers and took a little too long doing it. She stood up and grabbed her pink ball, a perky smile on her lips.

She knocked down a grand total of four pins. She cheered and came back to the food, downing half a cup of beer quickly followed by some hair-twirling and a giddy laugh.

I raised my eyebrows and gave Nate a look to see if we were seeing the same thing. He shrugged his shoulders at me as he shoved another nacho in his mouth.

It was Kent's turn. After his ball busted through all the pins he turned around and winked cockily at me.

I half smiled, my teeth biting the straw on my cup. "Oh it's on, Mr. Lytle," I said softly. He probably didn't even hear me but the threat was there.

Chapter 9

"My turn." Nate stood up and jogged to the lane. He grabbed a gold ball and lined up, he was super serious. He took his time and finally threw the ball down the lane. It looked like it was going well and then it went into the gutter.

"Booo!" I yelled.

While Nate waited for his ball to came back he grabbed the two pink balls and held them low, "Blue, er, pink balls!"

Jen whistled loudly. He chuckled, picking up the rest of the pins for a spare.

It was back around to me and when I got up to take my turn, Kent yelled, "Gutter ball!"

I looked at him over my shoulder and smiled. There hadn't been much to do all summer long in the small town my grandma lived in, except bowl and dance. I picked up my pink ball and chucked it down the lane. Another strike. I smiled triumphantly as I made my way back to the table. I winked at Kent and promptly stuck out my tongue as Kent did the same. I sat down next to Nate and fed him a nacho.

I rolled my eyes at Jen who sauntered up to get her ball and let her hips sway. Before I could turn away Jen picked up her ball and then dropped it. She giggled and bent over to pick it up. I felt bile rising in my throat. The jeans she was wearing were so tight I was amazed she could even get down that low.

I glanced at Nate out of the corner of my eye, he was watching but quickly looked away when he realized what she was up to. He smiled at me and opened his mouth for another nacho. I smiled, approving of his ability to resist Jen's backside, and fed him one as a reward.

I looked up at the scoreboard and saw that Jen had managed a strike. "Great job, babe!" Kent smiled proudly as he stood up. Jen leaned in and gave him a kiss, pulling back with his bottom lip between her teeth.

I wrinkled my nose and took a drink of water. I guess whatever shit they had been going through was over. If they wanted to play the PDA game I could play too. While Kent bowled I fed Nate more nachos and rehydrated. I was going to need it because Kent didn't like to lose and he wasn't going to go easy on me.

Kent got another strike.

After I matched Kent's strike, I pulled Nate with me to the jukebox. While we were looking for a selection he held me against him, cradling me against his chest, his hands resting innocently on my stomach.

After picking a couple of songs I turned in his arms and grabbed the front of his shirt, pulling him down so I could suck face with him. My body bent backwards as he held me close and kissed me senseless. Nate turned us around and pressed me against the wall, his hips grinding against mine, making my panties wet. My hands were in his soft black hair, gripping it tightly. His hands slipped under my shirt and mine slipped down to the bottom of his shirt.

Kent was there behind Nate and practically yelled us out of our love bubble, "Should Jen and I just go?!"

My lips peeled from Nate's as I froze in his arms. "Oh, sorry!" I pushed Nate away gently and touched my swollen lips. I smiled innocently to Kent though inside I was cheering myself on just a bit. My boyfriend couldn't keep his hands off of me and wasn't embarrassed to be seen with me. Score one for me.

Nate looked over his shoulder at the board, "My turn!" He ran off and bowled himself another spare.

"Sorry..." I said to Kent as I followed him back to the table.

"It's alright," he said as he stepped down to the bowling level and sat down next to Jen. She didn't make any effort to hide her hand which was running over Kent's thigh as he looked down the lanes at the other people. The intimacy she was showing him made something knot in my chest.

I turned my attention back to Nate, who was on his way over to me. He distracted me from my misery by kissing me gently. I smiled at him, "Thanks. Missed you."

I squirmed in my seat, my wet panties distracting me, "Be right back!" I got up and went to the restroom leaving Jen and Nate alone while Kent bowled.

When I came out of the bathroom I saw Jen was getting more beer and standing alongside Nate. They were talking together, Nate had Jen laughing.

I came up behind them and slapped Nate on the ass. "You're up!" Nate gave me another gentle kiss and then went to the lane, bumping shoulders with Kent on his way down. I glanced at the board and smiled. "Yay! I'm in the lead!"

Jen leaned over to me. "Good job. Nate is a hot one, girl."

"Thanks." I grinned and then coughed, wiping the merriment from my face as Kent came back. "Feeling a little...behind?" The score was quickly adding up for me and slowly adding up for Kent.

"Yeah. You'll fuck up eventually." Kent smiled sweetly as Nate threw his first strike.

Nate came back, checking Kent on his shoulder again, "Sorry, man." He put his arm around me and nibbled on my earlobe, making me squirm and giggle.

Kent nodded his head to Nate and pulled his eyes away from our PDA.

I ducked out of ear licking territory and stepped up to bowl. I had to wait for the other bowlers to go first so I looked around. I noticed that my shoe was untied and bent down to tie it. As I stood up I fell off balance and landed on my ass. I heard Jen snickering behind me. Nate helped me up. Kent probably thought that would be my black moment but it wasn't. Another strike for me.

I was still blushing as I walked into Nate's arms, burying my face against his chest. "So embarrassing..."

He held me and swayed gently, "No way, doll. No one even noticed."

"Yes they did!"

The game ended with me pounding Kent into second place. Followed by Nate and Jen, not that she cared because she was pretty drunk. Nate and I said goodbye to Kent and Jen after we returned our shoes. We walked home in different directions.

On the walk back Nate confided in me that Jen had hit on him when I was in the bathroom.

"Which time?"

"Both times! She was feeling up on my junk. I pushed her off but geez. That girl is a handful."

"She probably just accidentally brushed you or something." I refused to believe that Jen would openly grope my man, and in front of Kent no less!

* * *

The thought of Jen groping Nate had been on my mind all night and the next day when I sat down next to Kent in Art History class. I kept my eyes on my own notebook and didn't bother engaging with him.

As the professor walked into the lecture hall, Kent tugged on my hair and that's when I turned to him, and frowned. "What the hell?!"

He held up his hands in surrender, his expression irritatingly surprised. "Woah, Elly-beast. I asked you a question and you didn't answer."

"Yeah, well, maybe I just don't want to talk to you today," I snapped.

A flicker of a frown passed over his face before he shrugged and turned his attention to his notebook. "Okay. Sorry." He picked up his pencil as the lights went down.

I was trying to take notes next to him but his scribbling was getting on my last nerve. How dare he let Jen feel up my date. Was he in on it? Was it a little joke the two of them had going on between them? Or were they testing him?

At the end of class, after the lights went back on, I didn't move from my seat. Kent tried to step over me after saying excuse me but I pushed him back and stood up. "How could you let her do that?"

He looked at me, clearly confused, as he scratched at the back of his head. "Um..."

"Jen! You just sat there and watched as she groped Nate?"

Kent exhaled slowly and looked around at the stares turned our way. "Elly, this isn't the right place to talk about this."

"Fine! Fuck you too." I grabbed my things and made it down two steps before I felt his arm tugging me backwards.

"Elly, Jesus. Come on." He looked down at me with sympathy in his eyes. His hand slowly dropped back to his side. "She was drunk. I talked to her about it after she did it."

"After you left?"

"No, right after she groped him. I told her it was inappropriate and slutty and mean."

"Apparently she did it twice."

"I only saw the one time, Elly. That's the truth." He looked around, his cheeks blushing from the embarrassment of having to talk about this in front of prying eyes and ears. "Look, Jen's mom is divorcing her dad and it's been tough on her. Her trust fund is in jeopardy and she's been acting out."

"Am I supposed to feel sorry for her?" I raised my eyebrows in amazement at his audacity.

He shook his head and held up his hands defensively, "No, of course not. I just... I'm sorry. Ok? I'm sorry for her behavior. I completely understand if you don't want to be around her or bring Nate around her. But she isn't doing it to be mean to you."

I scoffed, "Yeah... okay. Keep telling yourself that."

"What am I supposed to do, Elly? Break up with her?"

I stared at him, wondering if he was really as stupid as he was acting. "Yes!"

He shook his head and looked away, his jaw clenching a couple of times before he looked back at me. "I can't do that. She'd had too much to drink, she wasn't herself."

I shook my head and rolled my eyes, "Oh, great. So anytime she wants to grope someone who isn't you she can just have some drinks and it'll be okay? That's the dumbest thing I've ever heard."

His ears burned red, "Just stay out of it, Elly. It's my relationship, not yours. I've been with Jen for years, not a few weeks."

I bit the inside of my cheek at his jab. "Fuck you." I turned and ran down the stairs, leaving him standing there.

JUST FRIENDS | 55

Chapter 10

I showed up to Thanksgiving dinner just before 3pm with a pecan pie on my hands. Not made by me, but my local grocery store. I couldn't bake to save my life. My mom had been over at Kent's mom's house since early that morning helping Kent's mom prepare the huge dinner as she did every year since we were eight or so. I dressed conservatively in a plain black dress that showed no bare skin below the neck or above the knee. My makeup, however, was the usual glossy lips and smokey eyes.

I made my way into the kitchen with the pie and set it down on the counter. "Hi Mrs. Lytle. It smells ridiculously wonderful in here."

Kent's mom glanced at me, she had a towel in her hand that she'd been using to dry the dishes and she brought it to her mouth in surprise when she took in my new transformation.

"Elly! Oh my god! Your mom told me you'd lost a little weight but this is...you look fantastic! KENT! Why didn't you tell me that Elly was a supermodel?"

I blushed and closed the distance, hugging Kent's mom briefly before stepping back. "Thank you, it's not a big deal."

I heard Kent from the living room. "Mom, I told you she looked good." In just a few seconds Kent came into the kitchen. I was still pretty pissed at him from our fight the week before. I'd been so pissed at him that I'd tried to switched sections in Art History just so I wouldn't have to see him. It hadn't worked.

"It is, dear, not a lot of people can accomplish what you have. And you!" she pointed at Kent, "You told me she looked good, I thought she got a new haircut or something. Not..." she swept her hand from my toes to my head. "This!"

While Kent and his mom bantered I held my breath and stared at Kent from across the room, studying him. I hated to admit that I didn't hate him. I didn't even dislike him, not even a little bit. The fact that he was supporting Jen, despite her bad behavior, just showed me how much he really loved her. For better or for worse he was going to be there for her. And I couldn't fault him for that.

"Elly's always been beautiful, mom. Or have you forgotten how you used to make me keep my door open because you were afraid we were having sex, huh?" He teased his mom and looked towards me and I looked away quickly.

"You two were inseparable. But I hadn't forgotten you constantly insisting that you and Elly weren't an item. You made it very clear you didn't have those feelings for her. But then Jen came along and I hardly saw you anymore." His mom raised her eyebrows. "I can only imagine what you two were up to at her huge, probably unsupervised, house and on those fancy vacations she'd treat you with."

Jen came in, a glass of wine already half consumed in her delicate hand, "Mrs. Lytle, you know exactly what we were up to. We were teenagers in love." Jen smiled up to Kent, wrapping her arm through his.

His cheeks started to turn a pale shade of pink as he shook his head. "C'mon Jen, not in front of my mom." He chuckled and ran his hand through his hair, releasing it from the gel cast that was probably Jen's doing.

I smiled politely as I shuffled my feet.

Jen bat her lashes at Kent, innocently. "What? It's not like she doesn't know about this stuff. She's a very smart lady. Even our little Elly..." Jen pressed her lips together and glanced between me and Kent.

I felt my stomach drop along with my smile. He'd told her

that I'd lost my virginity? He'd told her the horror story that was my first time? I looked down and tried to compose myself. He was in a relationship, did I really expect him to keep my secrets? I was a fool for thinking that he could.

Apparently she thought better than to bring up my horror story and went on a different path instead.

"Elly's been doing open mic nights at a local coffee shop. We haven't been able to make it but I've heard her name come up a few times between my circle of friends." Jen smiled softly to me and raised her wine glass in my direction. Her way of a peace offering, I guessed. Little did she know it was pointless.

Mrs. Lytle looked at me, "Yeah? I didn't know you read poetry."

"It's singing, mom. Elly sings. It's nice that she's finally doing it in front of other people."

I scoffed at Kent. "I sang in the car all the time."

Elly's mom came into the kitchen and rubbed Kent's back as if he were her own son. It perturbed me just a bit.

"It's true. And in her room. And in the supermarket. And at the doctor's office. She was always singing." My mom smiled at me, her face full of love.

I felt my cheeks heat and rolled my eyes, "We don't need to re-live my childhood right now. Do you need help with anything?"

Kent's mom looked around and shrugged her shoulders, "I had no idea you were a singer, Elly. You certainly never did it here. Not that I was eavesdropping or anything." She cleared her throat softly before continuing, "You could set the table, if you'd like, dear."

I nodded and stepped to the counter where the dishes were already stacked. "Excuse me." I grabbed the plates and silverware and smiled at Jen and Kent as I approached, I needed to get past them to set the table.

Kent moved Jen so I could squeeze by them. Just before I got passed I felt his hand on my arm and he pulled me into an awkward group hug. It was a bit weird being a threesome that way. It would be weird to be a threesome any way.

"Happy Thanksgiving, Elly," Kent said with a smile.

I winced as the plates and silverware smushed between us and tried to stamp down my anger at his chicanery. "Happy Thanksgiving to you too. Now let me go so we can eat, I'm starving!" I forced a grin that I wasn't anywhere near feeling and pulled away. My traitorous knees quaked slightly at his touch, which, I thought as I walked away, was completely ridiculous! I was losing it. Every since losing it I was even more aware of men and that included my off-limits friend.

As I was setting the table my thoughts turned briefly to Nate. It turned out I hadn't needed Kent's opinion of him after all. Two nights ago I'd asked him to come with me for my family Thanksgiving. He said he'd give me an answer the following evening. The answer had turned out to be a song he'd written for me called, "Let Her Go." I cried well into early that morning. I was still raw with emotion from the break up and I was sure that's why I was feeling all these things for Kent. It was transference or something.

After setting the table, I went out back to the swing that faced the garden and tall trees in Kent's backyard. I sat down and crossed my arms over my chest, getting some fresh crisp air, hoping it would calm down my raging libido and equally raging anger.

It wasn't long before I heard the back door open and the leaves crunch under someone's approaching feet. My tingling body told me it was Kent. And that only made me angrier.

"You alright, Elly?" Kent asked. I moved over as much as I could so he wouldn't be touching me as he took a seat beside me. "You seem...out of it tonight."

"Yeah, I'm okay. Just going through some stuff that I can't really talk to you about. And I'm pissed at you. I can't believe you told her. I..."

Kent was silent beside me. I looked down at my hands which were turned skyward on my lap. I wasn't sure what else to say. I still felt this wall coming between us, growing higher and higher. I knew that if I was going to remain sane I needed to try to distance myself from him. I couldn't let him get close so he could learn all my secrets and then blab them to Jen. She would torment me with them for the rest of my life or for however long she was in it. I didn't see an end in sight.

I looked up, staring out into the pretty little rose garden Kent's mom had planted a dozen summers ago. It was starting to lose its color as winter quickly approached.

I had come over every day to help Kent water them. His mother swore that they needed at least twenty minutes of watering every morning. I smiled to myself as I remembered the water fights we'd had as kids. It was so much simpler back then before the sexual tension arose and tried to drive me slowly crazy by dangling Kent in front of me morning, noon and night. That piece of cake I so desperately wanted but couldn't have.

Kent spoke softly beside me, breaking my thoughts, "You know she didn't think they were going to live. Everything else she planted died that year...even with her watering them daily to help them along. The roses, she decided to give the job to me, and then you joined in."

I chuckled softly, remembering, "She called them the Jesus roses." I forced my eyes to Kent.

I felt my shoulders hunch forward slightly, the smile at the corners of my eyes slowly dropped as I stared at him. My lips were dying to kiss his. And my brain wanted my hand to slap him, for being so stupid. With me and with Jen. My mind and body were at war.

Kent chewed on his lip as he continued to stare at the roses. "Have you ever wished you'd done things differently, Elly? Like there was something in your life that you weren't sure if you made a mistake or not?" It was a simple question but one that was laced, at least for me, with dozens of what-ifs. The what-ifs that would drive me crazy if I let them.

"Of course." I looked away, feeling guilty for thinking about wanting to molest him. "Don't you?"

"There are a few things that I think about a lot. I wonder what things would be like if things were done differently. I wonder what my mom would be doing. I wonder if she'd still be playing cards with your mom every Friday or if she'd be like one of those women who travels everywhere."

I looked at him again, the lust gone for the time being at the mention of his mother, whom he loved very much. "You mean if you hadn't scared all those guys away?"

"Yeah. I kept holding on to a hope that my dad would come back, but he never did. Do you think if I hadn't, that we'd be friends? Would my mom have ever met yours? When I think about it, I feel sad for my mom because I was a little shit, but the more I think about it, the more I'm glad I did because I can't see my life without you in it." Finally he took his eyes off the roses and looked at me.

I looked away, unable to hold his gaze when he was being so emotionally fluent. "We would've met in school." I shrugged my shoulders softly, it hurt to even begin to think about a life without him in it at all. It had been hard enough essentially separating from him since we graduated from high school. "You probably wouldn't have wanted to hang out with me though. But it doesn't matter, the past is in the past. You've been away at college for a couple years now and your mom could've found a man if she wanted to."

"Elly, I—," his words were interrupted by his mother shouting through the kitchen window that over-looked the back yard.

"Hey you guys, either water the roses or get in here and help eat some of this food!"

Kent turned his head towards the sound of his mother's voice as his resolve shattered, whatever he was going to say was lost.

"I think the roses are fine, maybe we should head back inside because she's not going to leave us alone otherwise," he said.

I nodded and stood up. I could stay mad at him or I could let go and pretend like we were ten again. I decided on the later. "I didn't come out here for the roses anyway, I'm famished." I put a hand to my flat stomach and then punched Kent on the arm. "Last one in has dish duty!"

I took off running before he was even on his feet and reached the door only a split second before he did, my cheeks flushed, my chest heaving lightly from the brief excursion.

"Mrs. Lytle, Kent said he'd love to do the dishes for you tonight after we finish eating." I giggled and smacked at Kent's finger as he poked me in my side. "Knock it off."

Everyone was already seated around the table. They saved an empty space next to Jen and a single plate across from them that was meant for me. They all looked at us as we approached the table.

Kent ran his hand through his hair with a chuckle since everyone caught him teasing me. And for a perfect moment it was as if the last four years hadn't happened and we were friends again.

"Sorry, we were just talking about the roses you planted ages ago, Mom," Kent said as he moved over and took the seat next to Jen, who wasn't smiling.

And as soon as I spotted Jen the moment was gone. I smiled at her, trying to reassure her that nothing fishy was going on, as I took my seat and put my cloth napkin on my lap. "The Jesus roses."

My mom laughed. "I haven't heard them called that in years. They were beautiful this past summer." She piled turkey on her plate and then passed the platter along.

"Those roses took lots of my time when I was younger, Mom. What did I do to deserve that, huh?" He asked with a grin as he took the platter from my mom. He put a generous portion of everything on his plate. He served Jen and then passed to his mother. I was the last to get the dishes as they were passed around.

Kent's mom snorted, "You used all the hot water every morning and you always got into the shower before I did, that's what you did."

Jen laughed, "Not much has changed. Kent uses up all my hot water too."

Kent smirked.

"So, Elly said you two have a class together? Art?," my mother asked innocently.

Kent froze for a moment before he put some green bean casserole in his mouth, "Yeah."

I could tell by his pasty complexion that he still hadn't shared that information with his girlfriend. He'd kept me a secret.

Jen looked at Kent with daggers. And those daggers would've sliced right through his whole body if they'd been real. She didn't verbalize anything, however, I was sure he'd get the verbal beating he deserved later on at home.

I tried to dispel the tension across the table, "Art History, mom. It's only like fifty minutes and we're really just sitting there looking and listening to the professor describe the slides. But Kent totally aced his midterm so I'm going to have to study with him for the final," I looked at Kent, "if that's okay with you, of course."

Kent chewed at his lip for a moment as he avoided looking at Jen. He nodded slowly, "Yeah. The mid term was easy, but the final is going to be harder. We'll try to get you a better grade on the midterm." Kent smiled sheepishly, probably embarrassed that he'd been caught lying about me.

Kent's mom looked at Jen, "Are you alright, dear?"

Jen's gaze switched to his mom and her fake-polite-happy face came back. She nodded, "Oh yes, is your stuffing homemade? It's delicious."

The small talk around the dinner table continued throughout the meal and it was centered on safe topics like politics and other worldly current events.

After dinner Jen volunteered to help Kent clean up the dishes. Before dessert could be served I grabbed my coat and made my way to the door. I paused and looked at our two moms. They had pulled out the photo albums and started reminiscing.

I smiled and cleared my throat, "Well, I'm going to head out. I'm working the dinner shift tonight..."

They glanced towards me and set the album down before coming over to give me goodbye hugs. "Elly, dear, it was so nice to see you. I'm still shocked by your transformation. You're still beautiful, but now it's easier for a stranger to recognize it."

"Thanks," I said softly.

My mom gave my cheek a kiss and then hugged me again. "I'll call you later."

"Okay, Mom." I peeked into the kitchen and waved from a distance, "Bye you guys, Happy Thanksgiving!"

Kent was standing there with Jen and judging by their body language they were in the middle of a whisper fight. Kent looked up and started to make a move towards me but Jen pulled him back. He raised his hand to me instead.

"Happy Thanksgiving, Elly. Thanks for coming."

Jen nodded her head as she gave me a courteous wave.

As I started out the door I looked back at Kent as he turned back around to finish working on the dishes. I noted that Jen's polite face was gone. Kent was going to get it good later. I only felt partially bad. He should've told her a long time ago. The confrontation he tried to avoid was coming back to bite him in the ass now. And he was a dick to me last week, so his ass deserved some punishment.

Chapter 11

Two days before finals I blocked Kent's exit after class let out. "So, I really need to study. Like today. Like, all day. And tomorrow... all day. Are you still going to help me?"

Kent looked up at me with a raise of his eyebrow. "So you're saying you want to cram as much as you can in the next little bit with hopes of getting a good grade, huh? I dunno, my schedule might be too busy." His finger came up as he tapped his chin and pretended to think. Kent's serious face made way for a grin as he nodded his head. "Jen went to go help her mom for a few days since she has to gather her things. She's moving to New York."

I exhaled a heavy breath. "Thank God! So can we study at her place then? My dorm room is...well, a mess and she has a whole apartment..." I bit my lower lip and looked up at him with huge kitten eyes.

"Elly, stop! Don't you," He scowled as he exhaled. "Those damn eyes get me every time. Alright, but we're gonna need cram food and drink. You know what that is. Don't worry, when we take a break we'll go jog around the apartment or something to burn it off."

I shook my head. "Uh-uh. There is very little sugar is in this tiny little body. I'll have water and carrots. I'll even bring them. And coffee, lots of coffee."

"God, Elly. When did you turn into such a health nut?" His finger snuck out and poked me in the stomach. I covered my stomach and took a step back. "Coffee will work, and I guess I can go without the sugar. Don't want to tempt you or anything."

"Tempt me all you want, I won't cave. I have excellent self control."

It hadn't always been so.

Kent raised his eyebrow and offered me that damn boyish grin of his. It made me want to swoon. I had to get out of there. I shifted restlessly as I waited.

"Alright. Fair enough. Give me a hour or so then meet me at her apartment?"

I nodded, grinning like I'd just won the lottery, which I had. He was going to make an excellent study partner, so long as there weren't any video games at Jen's apartment. "Sure, see you in an hour or so," I said.

* * *

After stopping at the grocery store for baby carrots, a huge bottle of water, and a bag of coffee, I knocked on Jen's apartment door. I braced myself, pretty certain that Jen would be on the other side, giving me the evil eye, and screwing up my study plans.

I exhaled a little breath of relief because when the door opened I only saw Kent in a pair of shorts, a tank top that showed the muscles he'd worked hard for, and his bare feet. He smiled, blocking the entry.

"Elly, I didn't expect you to show. I figured you'd be with Nate instead."

I narrowed my eyes at him and shook my head as I moved past him into the apartment, the plastic bag with the large water bottle was heavy and starting to turn my fingers blue.

He still didn't know that we'd broken up and I wasn't going to mention it. He'd pity me and I couldn't take that right now. It was better just avoid the subject all together. I blinked back the sting of tears in my eyes.

"You think I'd choose making out over studying for my art history final?" I asked, trying to keep my voice level.

There was a short pause as Kent shut the door behind me. "Well, yeah. I would." He chuckled and moved towards the dining room where he had his books and notes out.

I set my bags in the kitchen and then moved to the dining room table. I set my backpack in the chair and unzipped it as I pulled out my notes and stuff. I shook my head at his comment.

"I just...let's not talk about making out." I put my hand to my forehead and then moved my book bag to the other chair so I could sit down across from where he was set up.

Kent seemed a little confused for a moment, but he seemed to let it pass as he took his seat across from me.

"You know...it would be easier to cram if you could see my notes, because I take better notes. But if you want to stay over there I'll just push them over after I highlight them," he said.

I looked at him, staring at him for a good thirty seconds before huffing and standing up again. I pulled at the neck of my sweater to get air down my chest. "It's hot in here," I said as I sat down next to him and flipped my notebook to the beginning.

He stood up and walked over to knock the thermostat down a few degrees so the AC would turn on and blow some of that wonderfully chilly air out. When Kent returned he opened his notebook.

"We're gonna be going from Chapter 11 all the way to 22 for this final, mostly. There's going to be a few things from the first bit, but apparently the last half of the book is more important."

"Of course it is," I muttered, flipping my notebook until I found the right page. "Is that how you got your A last time? By making out instead of studying?" I had no idea why I was bringing up the making out again. I guess I wanted to torture myself. Or get it into my head that he was definitely, absolutely into his girlfriend. Which he was. Of course. I cleared my throat and kept my head down.

"I said I'd rather make out, not that I did. Wait, how did we get back to making out? I thought you didn't want to talk about it?" He was chuckling as he highlighted things in his notes in front of him.

I peeked over his forearm and frowned, pointing at something he highlighted, ignoring the fact that he'd totally called me out. "The professor never said that."

My breast was pressed against the back of his arm near his elbow. Kent looked at the thing he'd highlighted. For a moment he seemed to be lost. He was probably just thinking about making out with Jen. I pulled back from his arm and waited for his answer.

"He hinted at it so I made a note to research it. It's probably nothing, but I figured I'd be safe."

I scoffed. I was amazed how he could pick up on the professor's possible hints but not my own throughout the years. Maybe because the professor was a man. I nodded and leaned back, making a note of it myself.

"So was it bad?" I asked.

"Was what bad?" He highlighted some more.

"Whatever punishment Jen dished out for not telling her about Art History? It looked like she'd slapped you or something the first day we were back. Your face was all red." I continued making notes, highlighting what matched his, filling in what didn't. "Did she hit you?" I snuck a glance and noticed that his cheeks had turned a little red from the question.

I furrowed my brow. Did she really beat him up? If she did, I'd slap the shit out of her. I was about ready to protest when he spoke up.

"Jen gets a little physical sometimes." Kent took the time to chew on his lip. "Especially when she's drinking. But uh, no, she didn't hit me."

My pencil hit the notebook as I continued to stare at Kent's burning cheeks.

"What did she do to you then? I didn't imagine it."

Kent's eyes lifted from his notes and looked at the book on the table in front of him.

"It was a friction burn..."

"A friction burn from what?"

There was a short pause as his cheeks seemed to burn a little more.

"She held my hair with her hands and was grinding on my face with her..." His voice dropped out, leaving me to fill in the blank.

It was my turn to blush and I picked my pencil back up, "Oh.

Okay, next time just tell me that it's private and none of my business."

I started to write again, eyes moving between his book and mine. So she punished him with her boobs? First of all, that didn't seem like that bad of a punishment, Kent loved boobs. And secondly, how long would she have had to do that to leave a burn on his face?

My pencil paused mid-word and I looked at him again, the blush still present, "I didn't think boobs would leave that kind of irritation." I shook my head and looked back to my notes, "Hmm..." I finished the word and continued on.

"Not boobs," Kent blurted out, shaking his head. "Alright, I'm gonna grab some water and turn the AC down a little more."

I watched him get up, still trying to figure out what Jen would've done to him. I still hadn't figured it out by the time he came back to his seat. "If it wasn't her boobs then...?"

Kent pulled in a breath after he'd sat down and put the water on the table. "Her vagina, Elly."

I pressed my lips together, staring at the water and slowly nodded, "Right, yeah, of course, I'll be right back..." I got up and went to the bathroom, shutting the door behind me.

I stared at myself in the mirror, my cheeks were bright pink. I shook my head at my reflection, my hands gripping the sides of the counter. I whispered to myself, "Feel better now, Elly, now that you've bullied that out of him? Now you'll forever have the image of him with his head between her..." I cringed and felt my lunch rising up to my throat. It burned as I turned around and vomited in the toilet. "Oh god." I moaned as I flushed, my eyes closed against the contents being washed away. "Stop thinking about it..." I scolded myself softly.

There was a knock at the door, Kent's voice floated through it. "You okay, Elly? Do I need to hold your hair?"

I pressed my lips together, hoping he hadn't overheard me talking to myself. "Um...no, I'm fine. I'll be out in a—" The image came back into my mind again when I thought about hair and I bent over the toilet and vomited some more, it was louder this time, not much was left in my stomach at that point.

I heard the door open and Kent's feet padding on the tile floor as he came into the bathroom. He pulled the hair out of my face and held it with one hand as the other ran up and down my back. It was an annoyingly comforting feeling.

My hands were on the rim of the toilet, trying to hide what was in there from Kent's eyes. I flushed quickly and grabbed some toilet paper to wipe at my mouth.

"Kent, I'm fine, really." I said softly, throwing the paper into the water. My eyes were still closed, I wasn't sure I could do this. I wasn't sure I could look at his face. Maybe this was what I needed to finally be completely over him. He clearly loved Jen to let her do that to him. Especially long enough to leave a burn!

"You know how many times I've seen your vomit, Elly? It's no big deal. When you think you're done you can lay down on the couch for a little bit and I'll highlight your notes for you."

The soothing feeling of his warm hand on my back sent shivers up my spine and gave me goosebumps, I fought them back, chalking it up to the AC being turned on. I looked down at my sweater and cursed and when I caught sight of the vomit there I vomited again, retching loudly into the toilet. I moaned softly, "I need water, please."

Kent nodded his head and let my hair go. Oh god, how was I going to make it through the rest of the study session? I was going to fail this final, for real. I didn't have time to think anymore, he returned swiftly with a glass of water and held it to my lips. "Drink a little of this then you're going to turn around and we're going to get that sweater off of you. I got an extra shirt for when we get you out of that," he said.

I held the glass between my hands and tilted it back slowly, my eyes still closed, partly because I didn't want to see the vomit and partly because I didn't want to see him.

I heard Kent shuffle behind me and then felt his arms around me, I froze as his hands inched my shirt upwards.

"Lift your arms," he said softly. When I did he pulled the shirt over my head, careful not to spill the water still in my hand. He put something soft on my shoulder and then left the bathroom. "I'll go throw this in the washing machine."

I opened my eyes when I heard him in the kitchen and stared at myself, clad in only a pretty white bra with a gray male tank top draped over my shoulder. Even with the new body he didn't stop to stare at me or quiver when he was near me. I yanked the tank top off my shoulder roughly, pissed at myself for caring whether he was affected or not. Especially after...No! I wasn't going to think about it again.

I pulled the tank top on and then tied it at my side, making it fashionable and tight though the scoop neck was too large and showed off most of my bra, but that couldn't be helped. I came out of the bathroom after using some mouthwash and sat down at the kitchen table again after moving the chair to the other side of him.

"You should've given me one of Jen's sweaters. I'm small enough to fit in them now."

I heard the beep of the washing machine and then saw him coming back towards me. He grabbed another glass and filled it up at the sink with water, his eyes roaming over me for a long second. He was probably just looking for missed vomit or something. "Pfft, I think mine is a better look on you. Makes you look badass."

Kent's voice lowered as he dropped the glass off at the counter. "And sexy." It was almost too quiet to hear. Almost.

I raised my eyebrows, "What did you say?"

Kent seemed to struggle with himself for a moment. "I said, and sexy."

I stared at him and then shook my head to my shoulder, first on the right side then on the left, maybe I had blockage. "What? Sexy?" I blinked at him. "I just vomited in your toilet because..." I let that thought drop off, he didn't need to know the whys. "I just vomited in your toilet and you're saying that I look sexy?"

"I'm saying that you look sexy in my tank top."

I didn't want feel disappointed, but I was. He would say that about any good looking girl, and probably had to Jen on numerous occasions. I untied the knot at the side of the tank top, hopefully making it less sexy.

"Oh, right, well, thanks." I turned back to the table and hit his notebook with my pencil, avoiding his gaze further. "Come on, we're losing valuable study time."

He obeyed and came back to the table, "I'm sorry I got us off topic, it will be strictly business from this point forward. Now, let's review impressionism."

For the next few hours we studied hard. Very few times did we break from the studying. One of those times was when Kent put my sweater out to dry, the other was so he could brew some coffee several hours after sundown.

The information about how Jen liked to punish Kent was long forgotten as the history of art filled my brain. I was slowly dropping, my head on my arm sinking closer and closer to the page beneath it. "Kenny, so tired..." I said groggily.

Finally he stopped and closed his notebook. "Want to crash on the couch and we can start in the morning? I'll cook breakfast."

"Or here is good too." My head fell onto the notebook with a dull thud.

My eyes wouldn't open to see Kent but I heard him shuffling around and soon I felt like I was flying because he'd picked me up and walked me somewhere.

"You're not going to sleep in the damn chair at the table."

I leaned my head against his chest for the brief time I was in his arms. When I was laying on the couch I curled up into a little ball.

"It's cold."

It wasn't long before I felt something warm and fuzzy being draped over me. Another moment later I felt Kent kiss the top of my head.

"Sleep well, Elly."

It was the last thing I remembered before I slipped into sleep.

Chapter 12

In my dream Jen's vagina was coming towards my face. I fell violently off the couch and onto the hardwood floor.

"Ow, shit!" I whispered softly into the darkness.

I heard the thud of feet across the floor as Kent came rushing into the living room.

"Elly, you alright?"

I looked up and saw his bottom half wrapped in a blanket, his dark eyes staring down at me, concerned.

I felt heat drop to my breasts, my nipples tightened and I looked down, realizing the damn things were free, the tank top had turned sideways and somehow my bra had disappeared. I turned away from him quickly and grabbed the blanket I'd been given, covering myself with it before he noticed.

"Yeah, fine."

When I turned back to look at him I realized by the little look of surprise in his eyes that he'd seen. He looked away and heard him lick his lips.

"You were so tired I just put you on the couch. There is another bed if you'd like more room. It's full of clothes and shit but I'll put them somewhere else. I don't want you falling off the couch again."

"Okay," I got up and grabbed my bra from the back of the couch and then looked at him, waiting for him to lead the way. "Sorry I fell asleep on you."

"It's alright, Elly. Kind of reminds me of old times when you'd nod off at the computer." He winked as he turned around and took me to the guest room. He opened the door for me and scooped a pile of clothes off the bed. He put them on a chair in the corner of the room and then stepped back. "Want me to tuck you in, sleepy head?" Kent chuckled.

"Yeah, I do." I swept past him and crawled into the bed, flirting with him in my still sleep-laden state. I was being a smart ass and didn't expect him to follow through. Not the way I'd eluded to, anyway. He'd pull the covers up and kiss my forehead, of that I was sure.

And he did. He sat down on the bed next to me and pulled the covers up. But instead of my forehead he leaned down and kissed my cheek just a few inches from my lips. For a moment he seemed to hesitate. Or maybe it was just my imagination.

My stomach clenched at the intimacy. The near intimacy. "Why did you do that?" I whispered, staying deathly still under the covers, my words gushing out. The darkness of the room making me feel braver than I was.

Kent grabbed the blanket that had fallen onto the floor and rewrapped around his waist as he pulled a breath in and let it out slowly. "I...I don't know, Elly. I, uh...I'm going to go back to bed. If you need something just call..."

I sat up and grabbed for the top of the blanket at his waist, pulling him forward towards me in the darkness. I knew that this would be the only time I'd get this chance, the chance to feel his warmth in the bed behind me. I could close my eyes and pretend that he was mine.

"Wait, stay with me until I fall back asleep?" I pressed my lips together, hoping I knew him as well as I thought I did. I let go of his blanket slowly and laid back down, pulling the covers around myself again.

He stood there looking down at me for a long moment. When I was sure he was going to leave the room he nodded his head, "Scoot over." I watched him sit on the bed like I was a leper and felt tears prick at my eyes. So he would be in the bed with me but he didn't want to be close to me. What did I expect? I wasn't his girlfriend. I wasn't his cuddle buddy. I was just his friend and current study partner.

I closed my eyes tight and rolled over so my back was to him. I tried to clear my mind and then tried thinking about art history, baseball, The Bachelor. As soon as I saw the rose in my mind I felt his weight shift, and felt his warmth against my back. A few times when we were hanging out late in his room we'd fallen asleep on his bed and I'd woken up with him spooning me but it had never started out that way. My heart started to thud loudly in my chest.

I tried to clear the thoughts in my head that were suddenly turning dirty. I closed my eyes tightly and bit my lower lip. Oh my god, Elly. What are you doing? You seriously need to get laid.

I shifted a little, trying to see if he was aroused or just, being like a teddy bear. I could feel a little something, and as I wiggled I felt a little more. Oh shit. I bit my lower lip a bit more.

"You not comfortable?" He asked me as I felt him turn his lower half a little.

I reached behind me before I knew why I was doing it and put my hand on his leg to keep him from turning.

"I'm fine," I whispered softly. I removed my hand from his leg and slipped it back under the covers. I waited in the darkness to hear his breath deepen signaling that he was asleep.

I battled with myself internally on what to do next. Curiosity got the best of me and the little devil won out. I slowly, so slowly, lifted my arm from under the covers and reached it between our bodies, feeling for his crotch through his blanket and boxers.

Surprisingly, he was kind of hard, and larger than what I had remembered from when I caught him masturbating in his room so long ago.

I closed my eyes tight and held my breath as I stroked along the length of him, my thumb rubbing his tip gently. I wasn't sure what he'd do if he woke up, but apparently I was willing to find out. I could feel him growing more in my hand as I stroked him.

I pressed my thighs together as my insides started to flood with arousal. I slipped my warm fingers through the slit and wrapped my hand around him, squeezing lightly. I could feel him throbbing in my hand. His breathing hadn't changed yet, he appeared to be asleep still.

I stroked him a couple more times and then abandoned it for his hand. I pulled his hand slowly, softly until it was resting on the tank top's arm hole that was barely covering my breast. I closed my eyes and bit my lower lip hard to keep from moaning, his hand, so rough and warm was like ...heaven against my sensitive skin. Sparkling erotic heaven. I felt his hardness pressing against my backside and felt it throbbing as if it wanted out of the boxers. His breathing was unchanged.

I cupped the back of his hand and squeezed so that his hand squeezed my breast and then I reached back between us again, rolling forward a little so I could get my hand around him. I groaned and then bit my lip harder, punishing myself for being vocal. I felt him shift, but he only pushed his hips forward so his dick pressed against my ass with my hand still gripping it. My hand froze, while I waited to see if he'd awaken. His breathing went back to being steady once more.

I slipped from the bed slowly and then crawled back on it, next to him without the barrier of the covers between us. I closed my eyes as I put his arm back on my breast. And bit back another groan as I thrust my ass back against him.

I heard him in his sleep. Heard the little moan, but the breathing was still the same. I felt his hips starting to move in his sleep. He was so hard and throbbing.

I wasn't going to stop now, couldn't, even if I wanted to. I continued to rub him with my ass, clenching my thighs together as the dampness started to penetrate my jeans.

Another little moan came from Kent. I felt the little pulse of his hand closing and re-opening against my breast.

I moved my hand to the base of his head, my fingers threading into his dark hair. "Kent..." I moaned. He didn't stir, but moaned softly again. How far would it go before he woke up?

I turned my upper body so that I could press my lips to his. I kissed him softly, slowly. My fingers slid from his hair and moved over his ear, down his neck, slowly. "Kent..." I whispered again, my eyes half open and focused on his silhouette in the dark room.

His lips didn't change, they remained the same distance apart as I kissed him. His hips still moved here and there as his dick slid back and forth over my ass. I felt his hand give a little more of a squeeze to my breast.

I turned back and grabbed his hand, moving it down to my jeans. His hand had to be there in case he woke up and asked how the hell my pants got off. I quickly unbuttoned my jeans and slid them off, all with his limp hand in mine. When the deed was done and I was laying there in just his tank top and a pair of soaked white cotton briefs I moved his hand back up to my breast.

I sucked in a breath as I felt his hot length sliding against my cotton briefs. I felt it throbbing and felt those hips moving since there was stimulation again. It started to slide smoothly because of his own juices.

I bit my lower lip as I shifted again, moving up the bed a little higher. I reached between my silky thighs and grabbed onto his dick, pulling him down so that he was thrusting between my legs, rubbing my wet panties against my hot slit.

I felt him sliding back and forth between my thighs, feel his breath tickling my bare shoulder. His breath came out jagged and I swore I felt a kiss touch my skin.

I reached down between my legs and rubbed my swollen clit slowly, circling my middle finger around the nub. My breathing increased and a moan ripped out of me as I flicked myself with my finger.

"Kent..." I continued to stroke myself, my orgasm slowly building, "God Kent how I want you inside me..." I whispered, my thighs tight around his thrusting dick.

I felt another light kiss touch my shoulder and his hand again gripped my breast a little harder and stayed clinched this time, keeping the pressure there. He was slick with my juices and his own as they mixed. My breaths were short puffs of air as my body tensed, "Please, please, I need you inside, please," I begged quietly.

The hand at my breast moved down and stopped near my hip. Was he waking up? The excitement of that possibility made me groan. His hand at my hip slid down to one of the cheeks of my ass.

"Please..." I begged one more time.

That hand tucked under the back of those briefs and pulled them to the side. I felt his dick sliding against the wetness of my slit now. My breath hitched in my throat and my hand that had been between my thighs moved behind his head, gripping him in anticipation.

When his hips brought his dick back I felt the head touch to the lips of my slit. It was so wet. I felt him press forward with his hips.

"Yes," I moaned, gripping the back of his neck tighter. "Yes, Kent."

I felt his hips press forward more as he slid right inside of me, almost to the base. There was a gasp of breath from Kent. I was so wet, so tight. Only having had sex a handful of times before this time it was still new to me. My gasp matched his and my insides squeezed him.

A louder moan came from him this time and I felt that hand that had pulled my underwear to the side move to my breast. I gasped as he repeatedly filled me. The slowness of the act was different than my previous times and not unwelcome. "Kent, oh my god, so...good..."

I felt his body shift and felt him push me onto my stomach. His hands went to either side of me as he started to pump a little faster into me from above and behind me.

I was so relieved that he was finally inside me, sharing the most intimate part of myself with him. My hands went to the pillow, holding onto it tightly as he thrust into me. "Yes, yes..."

Those thrusts kept getting faster and faster. His lips touched my shoulder again as a little moan escaped his lips, the air brushing against the skin.

I gasped, "Kent!" I held on tight, and as if Kent knew what I needed, one arm shifted under me to lift me to my knees and he moved to his. Once more those thrusts started and I felt his hand slide between my legs. I felt his fingers rubbing back and forth over my clit as his thrusts pushed himself as deep as he would go.

My voice and body quivered at the same time as his expert fingers brought me home in a matter of seconds.

"Oh, fuck me!" My knees weakened and my hands clenched the bedsheets tightly as I released around him.

His finger didn't stop moving and neither did his dick as my insides squeezed him tightly. It wasn't long before his breaths were coming quicker. Just before he lost it inside of me he leaned back and pulled out. I felt his hot seed splash across my ass and part of my lower back.

I was too sated to care. My first ever orgasm during sex and Kent had been the one to rub it out of me. Who knew sex could be that good? I lowered myself onto the guest bed and slowly released the sheets from my hands. My breath recovered slowly. "Kent?..." I whispered softly.

Kent lowered himself to the bed beside me. I heard him mumble. "Mmhmm...? Sleep?..."

I looked over at him in the darkness, trying to see if his eyes were open. Maybe he was still asleep, maybe it wasn't unusual for him to be woken up with a sex offer from Jen when he slept over, maybe he thought I was Jen. I wasn't going to be able to sleep unless I knew. "Say my name..." I whispered again.

His eyes were closed, his breathing sounded like he was deep in sleep again as silence moved between us. There was no whispering of a name or movement from him.

I stared at him, watching him for a few more long minutes before I slowly got off the bed, careful not to roll over and get the bed dirty. I paused when I was off the bed and bit my lower lip, contemplating my next move.

If he was asleep and woke up and saw the bed clean would he be suspicious? Would he be able to smell me on him? I rubbed my forehead with my fingers, my face crunched up in anguish. I slipped my panties off slowly and then leaned over the bed, I almost wiped it onto the bed but then stopped. It would probably look staged. Oh shit, what was I going to do?

I ran into the bathroom near the front door and shut the door behind me. I threw the panties in the trash and then stared at them. I couldn't leave them there. Evidence. I grabbed the trash bag and tied it up tight. I put it by the door while I cleaned my lower back up. While I was staring at myself in the bathroom mirror I felt tears pricking at my eyes. What the fuck was I doing? I'd just seduced my friend, my very best friend since childhood. I was only mildly relieved that he wasn't going to know he'd had sleep sex with me. At least he wasn't going to have to carry that around with him. I washed my hands a few times and then grabbed the bag.

I went into the kitchen and pulled out half of the trash. I was glad her trash bags were white and not see through. I threw the bag in there and then covered it, burying the evidence. I padded back into the guest bedroom and grabbed up my jeans. I slipped them on, wincing because I was already sore from his girth. I pulled the tank top off. It was dark and Kent was asleep so I didn't bother hiding my body.

I went towards Jen's bedroom but thought better of it. I was too low to go in there. I was a home wrecker. A cheater. A hussy. I went into the living room and put the tank top on the couch arm. I put my bra back on and grabbed up my sweater from the chair where it had been drying. I pulled it on and then went back out into the living room.

I wrapped my arms around myself and looked around feeling terrible. So angry at myself for doing what I'd just done. I packed up my stuff slowly. The anger seeping from me in the form of hot tears.

Chapter 13

I knocked on Kent's door the next morning, a box of hot glazed donuts balanced on my hand. I was wearing black sweat pants, my Doc Martens, and our college logo on the front of my gray sweatshirt. My hair was up in a messy bun, no makeup on my face. I was trying whatever I could to look as unattractive as possible. It was the punishment for doing what I did last night. And if I was going to face him I needed to be sure I felt as insecure as possible so that I wouldn't try anything else.

Kent answered the door and offered me a smile as his eyes looked down at the box on my hand. "Donuts?" I could smell the fresh brewed coffee coming through the door.

"Yes. Good junk study food, right? And it'll go great with the coffee I smell." I raised my eyebrows and made the donut box levitate up to his nose.

Kent nodded, "I believe you are right." When the donut smell reached his nose he inhaled deeply and closed his eyes. "Just bring them in already, tease!" There was a pause. "Wait, donuts?"

I took a step forward and then stopped. "Yes,donuts...what's wrong with donuts?"

"I tried to get you to bring sweet stuff over last night and you brought carrots and water, now you show up with donuts?" He moved out of the doorway to let me come inside.

"And I was keeled over before half time. I thought we'd try your approach today." I moved to the counter and plopped the box down.

There was a nod of his head. "Alright, fair enough. I got lots of coffee and a frozen pizza in the freezer we can have later if you want." Kent shut the door and went to the kitchen. He got two coffee cups out of the cabinet.

"You want a cup to start with?" he asked as he poured a cup for himself and sat it on the counter. "We got a lot more to cover to get through it all."

"Sure, I'll have some." I unpacked my stuff, my back to him. "Did you talk to Jen this morning? I'm curious how the move is going."

"She hasn't replied to my messages. So I guess she's doing alright," Kent said as he poured another cup for me and brought them both to the table. His stuff was right where we'd left it.

I resumed my seat next to him. "She probably heard through one of her groupies that you had a girl over last night." I sipped the coffee slowly not wanting to burn my tongue too badly if it was too hot. I was waiting for him to bring it up, to bring up that I'd left without saying anything. To bring up that we'd had sex last night and that he remembered. Anything.

"Groupies? That's a high comment for her." He pulled his seat in a little. "I think we left off at Cubism."

But he didn't mention any of that. He just pushed forward as if it had never happened. And so I'd do the same. Because I was the worst kind of person. A cheater. And I'd drug him down with me.

"Cubism?" I pinched my forehead as I tried to refocus my mind on the studying. "Did we even cover that in class?"

He nodded again. "You were snoozing a little that day. Doodling. I figured we'd study sometime and we'd cover it. See. I'm good for something." Kent grinned.

"Of course you are. Studying and," I chuckled, "distracting."

"Distracting?" He flexed the muscles of his arm. "I had no idea." He laughed as he picked up his highlighter.

I rolled my eyes at the arm flex. Jesus, why did he have to be so tempting? Was he flirting with me on purpose or just doing it a normal amount? My mushy brain couldn't tell anymore. "I wasn't talking about your body, you nerd. I was talking about your video gaming and stuff."

"Forgive me, Miss Sexy Ass," he said with a chuckle and highlighted a large passage in his notebook.

I clenched my jaw tight and started writing the large portion that he highlighted. Kent commenting on my sexy ass was not something I wanted to think about, especially since he jizzed all over it last night. My cheeks started to blush as I remembered. I tried so hard to push it out of my mind and focus on the studying at hand.

We covered a lot of things in the next few hours. Kent's damn near perfect notes were sinking into my brain with the help of coffee and a little bit of sweets.

I groaned and put my pencil down. I shook my hand out and let out a whimper. "I've never written so much in my life! Can we take a break now?"

He slowly put his pencil down. "More coffee?" He stood up.

"Yeah."

"Let me get rid of the old coffee first," he said, moving to the kitchen.

I went to the bathroom and then into the living room. My back was sore from bending over the table all morning so I stretched, grabbing my calves one at a time, my body bending in half. I stood up straight, stretched out my arms and back and then rejoined him at the table. I took the donut from his hands just before it reached his mouth and then put it to mine. "Yum!"

"What the hell?" He turned his eyes on me. "I'm going to get that back."

I took a bite and talked around my chewing. "Mmm, 'o 'ood!"

He smirked. "I'm warning you. I'm going to get it back."

I stuffed the donut in my mouth as quickly as I could.

And I had most of it in my mouth when he pounced on me. An arm tucked around me and pulled me against him and he stood up so my feet dangled. His other hand was trying to get the rest of the donut out of my hand before I got all of it in my mouth. I screamed as best as I could and tried to keep the donut away from his hand, holding it out.

"Mmm!"

"Gimme the donut, woman!"

He grabbed my arm and tried to pull it down. I kicked at his knees lightly with my toes, not really wanting to hurt him and stretched upwards with all my might to keep the donut away from him.

Finally having swallowed what was in my mouth I retorted, "Never! It's my donut now!"

"I don't think so!" The grip around my waist slipped and I slid down against him an odd number of inches so that my face was almost across from his.

Because of what happened last night my composure started to slip as the memories of him pumping into me invaded my mind. I stilled in his grasp. I shoved the remaining bit of the donut in his mouth and then pushed at his chest so he'd release me.

"Fine! Have my sloppy seconds, I don't care," I retorted, trying to sound much more badass than I felt.

He let me down quickly. There was a moment that his eyes weren't looking at me, but they shifted towards me as he smiled. "Vic'ory!" came from his full mouth.

I rolled my eyes and then sat back down, I ate most of a donut so I wasn't going to get another one. I couldn't clock an extra hour at the gym at the rate the studying was going. I sipped my coffee and picked my pencil back up. "Barely," I muttered to my notebook.

Kent picked up his cup of coffee to help get the rest of the donut down. "I was going to win and you know it!" He reclaimed his seat next to me.

"By cheating, of course, just like you always do." I sniffled once like I always did when I wanted to show that I was better than him.

A smirk showed on his face as he picked up his highlighter. "Just remember who's helping you ace this final, Elly."

"I haven't aced it yet."

"But you're going to." Kent started highlighting things again.

I grabbed his highlighter and stuck it under my thigh. "I need to catch up. Hold on a minute."

Kent's hand rested on his notebook as his eyebrow raised. His eyes shifted to where I sat and the leg his highlighter was under. His eyes closed as he got some more coffee.

"Fine, fine."

I wrote slower now that I was in control, a small smile of victory on my lips now. Kent took a sip of coffee and then smiled at my antics. I started to hum, waiting to see how long it would be until Kent said something about my new, much slower study approach.

He let me write like that for a few minutes before he spoke up. "You know, today is the last day we have to cram stuff."

"Mmmhmm. I'm well aware." I didn't look up from my turtle-slow pencil.

The muscles of his jaw tightened. The fingers of his hand thumped on the table. His hand hesitated.

I noted his body language and had hidden enough things from him over our lifetime that I knew he was about to reach for it. I grabbed the highlighter and sat on it, only the very end of it visible under the crotch of my sweatpants. I smirked, no way was he going to go for the vag.

Kent watched me shift around and stared at my crotch. "You think it's safe there?" The muscles of his jaw tightened.

I paused in my writing and studied his face, narrowing my eyes. My own jaw clenched. I grabbed the highlighter out, turned my back to him, shoved it up my shirt and under my bra, safely nuzzling it against my right breast. He'd have to touch it to get the marker back.

"There. I think Jen would be pretty upset if I told her you groped my breast." I smiled smugly.

His lip twitched which happened when he got agitated. "That's nice. Using the girlfriend against me. You know what. I don't think you will." His hand moved from the table as he went for the highlighter.

I grabbed him by the wrist and held him back, two inches from my boobs and looked him in the eye. "You really think that's wise?"

I knew I shouldn't stare him down this way and have the undertone of what happened last night be out in the open but he was playing with fire. My fire. And I didn't appreciate it. Sure, I'd kind of started it but he should be backing off, not trying to grope me.

His eyes looked into mine as I held his wrist. The muscles of his jaw tightened and loosened and finally he spoke. "Whatever..." He pulled his wrist from my hand and stood. He moved towards the bathroom.

I exhaled a held breath after he was gone from view. I pulled the highlighter out and hid it under his book and then I started writing at super speed again so that I would be caught up when he came back.

Kent was gone for a little while. About fifteen minutes passed and he finally came out of the bathroom wrapped in a towel. He moved towards Jen's room to get a change of clothes.

I caught sight of his towel clad body and heat stirred between my thighs. I pressed them together and cleared my throat loudly,

"What the hell, Kent? Had to clean the image of you touching my boobs out of your mind?" As soon as I said it I knew it hadn't come out the self-degrading way I'd meant it to come out.

Kent looked at me for a moment and stuck his tongue out at me. I felt my body relax, he had taken it the way I'd intended.

"Not hardly. I needed a shower. I figured it would give you time to catch up."

I nodded. "Carry on then." I looked down at my notes and put my pencil down. I was caught up and had even moved ahead a little, copying the things I knew for sure he'd highlight. I wasn't dumb. I didn't even really need to study with him I could've just borrowed his notes for a few hours. I got up and refilled my coffee. I wrinkled my nose at the taste and decided to brew a fresh pot.

Kent came out a few minutes later with fresh clothes on. He raised his eyebrow at me, leaning against the counter. "I guess you caught up then."

"And then some." I turned so my butt was pressed up against the counter behind me, "Want your highlighter back now?" I put my hands on the counter too and arched my back, my breasts, small as they were, puffed out.

Kent's eyes were drawn to my breasts which were poked out now. His eyes shifted away from them as his cheeks started to show a blush. "It's not there. I can see there's no outline like before."

I looked down at my chest and then at him, frowning. "How can you make out the outline of anything under this huge sweatshirt?"

"Because when you shoved it in there earlier you could see the way it was held under the strap of your bra." So he apparently was checking out my breasts.

"You need your girlfriend to come back so you can get laid. You're a little pervy." I turned my back on him as I refilled my mug with fresh, hot coffee.

I couldn't believe I was shoving my boobs at him. He wasn't the only one who needed to get laid. I was acting like a dog in heat. I needed to reign it in.

He closed the distance between us after he emptied his mug in the sink and forced his way to the coffee pot with a bump of his hip. I jumped back as the coffee sloshed out of my mug.

I held it out just in time to avoid a burn, "Jerk!"

I went back to the table and on my way I grabbed a wooden spoon from the jar of utensils on the counter and slapped his ass with it. The sound of the spoon cracking against his pants echoed in the kitchen.

Kent jumped. "OUCH!" He put the coffee cup down and his hand moved to rub the place I'd hit. I bit my lower lip, wondering if maybe I'd gone too far as I eyed him from the safety of the chair I'd run back to. Kent turned half his body and his hand pulled the back part of his shorts down. An red angry welt in the shape of a spoon stared at me.

"I'm surprised you can see it so well through all your ass hair." I pressed my lips together, trying not to laugh.

"What the hell are you talking about?" he said as he mooned me. "Look at that!"

I couldn't help it, a chuckle burst out. "I see it! Now put that thing away!" I held out a hand, trying to block his ass from my view.

Kent pulled his shorts back up as he grumbled on his way back to the table, coffee cup in his hand. He took a seat, wincing until he settled in.

I glanced down at the front of his shorts, maybe Kent was into that kind of thing. He looked at my face and saw where my eyes were pointed. He looked down. "Is there something on my shorts?"

"Er...um, no!" My cheeks turned pink at being caught staring at his crotch. My eyes turned back to his notebook. "I'm just gazing off waiting for you to highlight some more."

Kent looked up at me as he saw my eyes shift. Kent shook his head and picked up the highlighter.

Several more hours of intense studying went by and then the front door opened and Jen came in.

"Hello?" she called as she closed the door behind her. She came towards the kitchen and smiled softly at the two of us, I knew I looked ragged and it probably pleased Jen to no end. "Still studying?"

Kent looked up from the notebook, smiled and nodded. "Yeah. Been at it for hours. There's some coffee, but it's not too fresh. There's a few donuts left too. How was the move?" He put the highlighter down to give her his full attention.

I stopped for the moment too, eyes on Jen. Jen looked flawless, as usual. She rolled her bag to the hallway that led the master bedroom and then removed her coat.

"It was good. Therapeutic for mother, I think. Are you going to be studying for much longer? I was hoping we could go out to dinner with Courtney and Reed tonight."

Kent looked down at the notebook. "We got a few more chapters to cover. You can maybe go out to meet them and I'll join you after we're done?"

She smiled softly and nodded. "Sure, darling."

She put her coat into the coat closet and then grabbed her bag and disappeared with it into the master bedroom. I hoped the blush didn't make me look suspicious. When I saw Jen my mind instantly went to the moments I'd shared with Kent last night and the guilt set in.

Kent watched her go into the bedroom with a raise of his eyebrow. There was apparently something on his mind, but I had no idea what. I cleared my throat softly and looked back to my notebook, resuming copying the notes. "I can probably just do the last chapters by myself. I don't want to hold you up."

He looked back down to the notebook and picked up the highlighter. "No. We started this, we're going to finish it."

I couldn't be in the same room with them. I couldn't sit here and pretend that Jen wasn't in the other room. The Elly and Kent bubble was broken. If I stayed any longer I was likely to burst into tears because of what we'd done - what I'd done. As far as I knew he thought it was a dream. And that's how it would have to stay. A beautiful dream that would never be repeated.

I silently packed up my books. "Kent, my energy is depleted, I'm going to go back to the dorm and nap for a little while and then pull an all-nighter. I'll see you tomorrow at the final, ok?" I didn't look at him, not wanting him to catch my glossy eyes.

"But..." He tried to look at me but I kept moving so he couldn't catch my gaze. Kent sighed, shut his notebook and pushed it into the bag I was packing. "Take it. I highlighted the rest you'd need so you shouldn't have to pull an all-nighter."

I took it because I didn't want to argue with him. "Thanks. I'll see you later. Sorry for being a pain in your ass, literally." I zipped up my bag and quickly left, not giving him much of a chance to respond.

Chapter 14

It was the first time in a long time that I was excited for Christmas. Kent had spent the past two Christmases somewhere warm with Jen's family, but this year he'd decided to stay and participate in his usual traditions. One of them was spending Christmas Eve doing puzzles, watching horror movies, and eating junk food with me while our moms went to their annual Christmas party at Mrs. Frederick's house.

Mrs. Frederick had been throwing the same Christmas Eve

party for the past sixteen years. She hosted the first one when she was a nineteen-year-old newlywed and it had grown from a single couple into one of the most talked about events in my mother's circle of friends throughout the years. My mother was upstairs getting dressed for the occasion, which she had been talking about ever since I got home on Christmas break, three days ago.

I, on the other hand, was very much looking forward to snuggling under a blanket with Kent's shoulder touching mine. I couldn't wait to be so close that so that I could smell him again. I didn't wash my hair for three days after we'd studied together just so that I could still smell him on my body, somewhere.

I'd had visions that morning of him feeding me carrots, holding me to his chest, stroking my hair. And just as we'd finished the last movie we'd kiss, in the dim room, lit only by the twinkling Christmas lights and the rolling movie credits.

"Mom! He'll be here any minute!" I was standing in the kitchen, preparing a large tray of veggies and dip. My excitement was palpable and I could barely contain it.

"Give me a minute, Elly! Geez. Why do you have such a bug up your butt?" she called from upstairs somewhere.

I wanted to see Kent. That was the bug up my butt. I hadn't seen him in almost a week and a half, since our final, and I'd been thinking about him non-stop since that night we'd shared together.

I jumped as a knock sounded at the door and ran to answer it. I made sure my clothes were properly in place before opening the door. Kent was there, my heart skipped a beat as I stared at him.

"Hey," I said casually. I hoped he wouldn't notice that I was nervous and giddy.

He flashed me a smile as he held up a couple of plastic bags. "Brought some stuff."

"Great." I stepped back to let him in and just as I was about to shut the door behind him I felt resistance on the other side.

"Not so fast, Elly. Don't forget about me." Jen smiled sweetly as she stuck her hands in the back of Kent's pockets. As they walked through the foyer she pressed a few loud kisses to the back of his neck.

I felt my heart drop in my chest and jealousy color my face. What the hell was she doing here? "Uh..." I shut the door and racked my brain for words, any words, as I stared at them.

My mom came down the stairs, all dressed up, and frowned at me before grabbing her own coat from the closet. "Elly! Don't be rude. Take their coats and offer them something to drink. Don't just leave them standing there." She kissed my cheek, grabbed her keys and left us there, alone.

I shook the shock from my face and pasted on a polite smile. "Yeah, sorry. Let me take your coats, I'll hang them up for you."

Kent sat the bags down, and offered his coat to me. Jen took a minute before she removed hers. She was wearing a low cut v-neck sweater, showing off her perfect cleavage. Kent smiled as I took it. "Thanks. " His eyes passed from Jen to me before he picked the bags up. "I'll go put this in the kitchen," he said.

I nodded as I watched him disappear into the kitchen. Jen had no problem letting me serve her, she held it out to me with a grin. Once he was gone Jen looked me over slowly, "You look...nice." Her voice was dripping with sarcasm.

Had I known that Jen was going to be here and flashing everyone maybe I would've worn something flashy too. But no, I thought, probably not. It was a lounge around night. I was dressed for comfort, not to impress. If I had her boobs maybe I'd wear a deep v-neck too. I squeezed my contempt and stuffed it deep down as I turned around, hanging up their coats in the closet.

"Thanks," I managed to get out. I think it even sounded slightly polite.

Kent returned from the kitchen, clapping his hands and then rubbing them together as he looked between us. "We're set with drinks, snacks and board games. Did you get some puzzles, Els?"

Jen shrugged her shoulders happily as she slid next to Kent and wrapped her arms around his middle, hugging him to his side. "It's going to be a fun night!"

I smiled coldly, "I did. But maybe since Jen is here she'd like to do something less nerdy. What board game did you bring? Candyland?"

A playful smirk moved along Jen's glossy lips. She shook her head which caused her breasts to press against Kent. "I was thinking we could do something else. Maybe strip poker. "

He ran his hand through his short hair, his other arm around her, holding her against him as he tried to break the tension between us. "We can watch a movie now and figure out the rest later."

"Great. It's settled. You guys go get comfortable in the living room. I'll bring in the snacks for the movie." My back was stiff as I walked away from them. I heard her giggling as they walking into the living room. The cabinets were banging a little louder than normal as I tried to work off some of my frustration.

I had to make a couple of trips back and forth to the kitchen. The first trip back, I saw Kent and Jen snuggled up together on the couch I let the snacks fall loudly on the coffee table. When I came back again I had water bottles. I tossed two roughly at Kent's crotch and held onto the third. The first bottle was caught but the second connected with his thigh, making Kent jump. He coughed from the close call and frowned at me.

"Do you want to watch The Zombie Who Stole Christmas or Miracle on 34th Street?" I asked.

"The Zombie Who Stole Christmas," he said.

Jen spoke softly, giving him the little girl talk again, "But Ken..." I clenched my jaw at her nickname as I waited. "It's going to be scary."

"Don't worry, I won't let any zombies get you." The arm around Jen snuggled her in closer as he pressed a kiss to her forehead.

I turned around and put the DVD into the player. I set my bottle of water down on the floor and went to the recliner where the blankets were waiting to be used.

I grabbed both of them and shook them out a little. Two blankets, three people. Damnit. I heard my mother's voice in my head scolding me for not giving my guests their own blankets. I tossed them both onto the couch next to Kent and then sat down on the floor in front of the coffee table, ostracizing myself.

I kept my eyes forward on the TV as the credits started and then everything went black as a blanket was thrown on my head. I frowned, grabbed it and threw it back at him. He didn't catch it because he was in the middle of spreading out the other blanket over him and his girlfriend.

"If you want it back, let me know," he said as Jen snuggled into his side, her hands hidden by the blanket.

I grabbed the veggies and turned around again. Fifteen minutes into the movie and I heard Kent's breath catch behind me. Seriously? I forced myself to keep staring at the TV. I would not turn around. I would not turn around. I would not—

A zombie killer came out of nowhere leaving me and Jen screaming.

I heard Kent chuckle and then some whispering from Jen and then another chuckle. There was snow and blood all over the screen and suddenly I was feeling very cold. I turned around and spotted Jen's hand pumping up and down under the blanket. Eyes wide I quickly pointed to the blanket beside Kent. "Can I have that, please?"

Kent shifted a little and the motion paused. "Yeah," he said as he tossed me the blanket. I caught it and wrapped it around myself as I got back into position. I leaned forward and turned the TV up before settling in, munching celery as zombies snacked on human flesh.

"Ewww," I heard Jen's annoying voice behind me. I rolled my eyes and tried to block her out for the remainder of the movie.

As the credits started Jen excused herself to go to the bathroom and Kent remained carefully hidden under the blanket. I turned around after she left and got up onto my knees, grasping the coffee table in my shock, "Kent Matthew Lyle!" I whisper yelled, "Did you just let her...? Did she?..." I felt like my eyelids might stay stuck open forever if they went any wider.

He shook his head. "I didn't let her get that far. " he said softly.

"Liar," I continued to whisper as I got up and moved to the couch. No way was there that much noise and giggling and whispering without Kent getting his rocks off.

Kent had the blanket over him still. "Not lying." I sat down next to him and pulled the blanket down so I could see. His pants were still zipped, the outline of his hard penis straining against his pants. He yanked the blanket back over himself with a blush. "Geez, Elly."

"Gross, Kent," I scolded him again in a hushed voice as I moved away from him. Mad that I wasn't the one who'd given it to him. Madder still that Jen had done it, in my house! While I was in the room! I snatched up the snacks and glared at it, "It's Christmas for Christ's sake," I said over my shoulder as I took the snacks to the kitchen.

By the time I came out of the kitchen Jen and Kent were at the front door, shrugging themselves into their coats.

"Leaving already?" I tried to leave the disappointment out of my voice. I wasn't sad for Jen to be leaving. But for Kent, my heart squeezed tightly. And I hated that it did. He was blatantly letting his skanky girlfriend disrespect me in my mom's house.

"Yeah," Kent said as he avoided my eyes, "Jen's mom invited us to dinner. So we've got to run."

He was lying. But I wasn't going to call him out on it. If he wanted to leave, he could. I wasn't going to force him to stay in my company for any longer than he wanted to...which didn't seem to be very long at all.

I nodded and waited for them to step through the door. "Cool. Well, Merry Christmas." I watched as they stepped down to the sidewalk. Kent briefly waved, still avoiding my direct gaze. Jen, on the other hand, she waved and smiled cheerfully, almost as if rubbing it in.

"Merry Christmas, Elly! Have a good night! Don't forget to go to bed early so that Santa Claus can come!" She disappeared into Kent's SUV after he shut the door. He glanced at me from a distance, held his hand up in parting and then disappeared from view himself.

I felt the sting of tears in my eyes as I shut the door. Great. I was all alone. I wasn't going to let myself wallow in my self-pity, however. I was going to a party. A grown-up party. With adults who probably wouldn't be wanking each other off underneath their hosts' blankets.

Best case scenario there was another lonely soul there like myself. Worst case scenario, I'd get really, really drunk, for free.

Chapter 15

I stopped by Stacy's house and picked her up. She would be my partner in crime tonight. The best case scenario was already under way as we stepped in, together, to Mrs. Frederick's party.

The cacophony of voices was overwhelming and bodies were everywhere. Mrs. Frederick was standing by the door and smiled at us as we entered, "Elly, dear. You've finally come to my Christmas Eve Bash!" She touched my shoulder lightly.

I smiled politely and nodded, "Yes, ma'am. And I brought a friend too, I hope you don't mind."

She wrinkled her nose and shook her head, her smile still on her lips. "Oh, no, of course not. Make yourselves at home. There are a few other younger people here. I think they're downstairs with the karaoke. Go ahead and put your coats in the laundry room and then head on down there."

I looked behind me to Stacy, who nodded, and then turned back to Mrs. Frederick and smiled. A shrug of my shoulders and we were off. We left our coats on the rack and then proceeded downstairs after a doing a loop and finding nothing else interesting.

We were greeted immediately to the overwhelming smell of pot and the soft thumping of bass-heavy dance music. I coughed and waved my hand in front of my nose as we made our descent. Stacy leaned down and whispered into my ear, "You've never smoked before?" She sounded almost giddy at the realization.

"No! And I don't plan on starting now, either."

There was a group of five sitting on the couch. A blonde guy on the end was taking a hit off a green bong while the others watched. I wondered if karaoke was code for getting high. If it was I wasn't sure I was wanting to participate.

I recognized one of the girls. She was a close friend of Jen's and as soon as my eyes locked on her I felt my stomach clench. She recognized me too and pointed her candy red nail directly at me, "Hey! I know that girl! Hey, girl! Come on over here!" She smacked the boy who was sitting next to her. "Make some room!"

"Watch it, Sadie," he warned before moving over. A couple got off the couch too, to make room. I walked over slowly and sat down next to Sadie with an apprehensive smile. I felt like this was a trick.

"Hey... Sadie."

"How do I know you?" She wrapped her arm around my shoulder and pulled me in close.

"Um... Jen, I think." I looked at Stacy, who had sat down beside me, but she was busy staring at the bong and asking twenty questions about the pot inside of it.

Sadie yanked on me, causing me to give her my full attention. "Oh yeah! You're the girl who is always trying to steal her boyfriend." She laughed and I smiled, though I didn't think that was very funny.

"I'm not really trying to steal him. We are just friends."

She laughed again. "Oh, sure, sure. I tried to steal him too until I realized what a geek he was, no worries."

I laughed mirthlessly and pulled away, "Yeah..." I turned my attention to the coffee table. It was a smorgasbord of junk food and the only thing that looked even slightly appealing were the brownies. I shook my head, I wasn't going waste my calories on some stupid brownies, and looked up just in time to see Jen's long legs coming into view as she came down the stairs.

Sadie looked too and gasped with excitement when she saw Jen. "Hey, girl!!" She jumped up and ran to her, wrapping her up in her weirdly strong embrace. Kent was behind her and I looked away before he could meet my gaze. Maybe if I just chilled here and looked away he wouldn't notice me. Maybe I could camouflage myself into the couch.

Nope. No, I wasn't that lucky. "Hey, Elly," he said, sounding surprised.

I saw Stacy look up at Kent because I was looking at her. She looked at me and cocked her head towards Kent to try to get me to say hi.

I looked up and gasped in surprise. "Kent! Wow! Crazy seeing you here since you said you were going to be with Jen's mom all night tonight." I heard the blonde guy bust out in laughter. When I replayed what I'd said it had definitely come out wrong.

Kent cleared his throat, and his shoulders were rigid, probably because he thought the blonde guy was making fun of him. "Crazy seeing you here too, since I thought you'd be at home playing with yourself tonight," the corner of his lips kicked up just a bit.

I glared at him as the blonde guy all but rolled on the floor in his joy. Stacy chuckled too for a few seconds, but quickly cleared her throat to stop herself. She grabbed the bong and took a big hit.

"I'll be right back." I stood up and moved past the couple making out on the couch. The boy had his hand way up her shirt and I couldn't help but feel a tiny bit jealous. It should've been me and Kent on a couch making out. But no. He was here with her.

The bar was tucked back in the corner and I looked over the bottles as I tried to devise a plan to get Kent to realize he had feelings for me. If nothing else I could declare my love for him. But what if he rejected me? What was I saying? He probably would reject me. He definitely participated in the sleep sex. Your body doesn't just do that and grope people when you're unconscious.

I poured whiskey into a red plastic cup and took a big gulp. It burned on its way down and caused me to cough. I felt a warm hand slapping me gently on my back. The tingles and prickles I felt going through my body told me it was Kent before I even turned around.

"Easy, Elly. Whiskey is risky." He grinned at his own rhyme. Upon seeing my grimace his lips turned down in a frown. "Fine. Don't think I'm cute tonight. But this is a mistake." He took the plastic cup from me and set it down on the bar behind me.

I turned around and picked it up. I gulped it down and then slammed the plastic cup down on the bar. I met his gaze and there was silence between us as I tried to keep my whiskey down. "The only mistake was..." I pressed my lips together to keep from saying it. If he didn't know then he'd probably think I was being jealous or spiteful. If he did know then my heart would be crushed when he confirmed it was a mistake.

"Was what?"

"Was inviting you over for Christmas Eve."

He looked as if he'd been slapped and I left him that way. I realized halfway back to the couch that I forgot the whiskey. Kent had moved back to Jen, his face still pale. I huffed to myself. I was glad he was feeling some of the pain I'd felt earlier. Served him right for ruining our tradition. I topped my cup off and then joined Stacy on the couch.

"Want some?" I held my cup under her nose so she could smell it. She turned away with disgust.

"God, no! Why would anyone want that? I want Schnapps." She looked over one shoulder and then the other and then back to me. "Did they have Schnapps?"

I shrugged my shoulders. "I have no idea. I just picked up the prettiest bottle."

Stacy gave me an odd look and then shrugged. "Ah well, I'll have something later." She settled back against the couch and sighed happily, "I have a good buzz going right now."

"Why do you smoke pot? It smells like shit," I said. "Like, literally, shit."

"So does that shit." She pointed to my cup.

I held it to my nose. It burned but it certainly didn't smell like poop. "It does not!"

She grinned. "To each their own."

Kent and Jen slowly made their way over to the couches. Jen took a hit off the bong and Kent stayed next to her, rubbing her back as he stared off into space. Every once in a while she'd pull him into the conversation but he was somewhere else.

I finished off my second cupful of whiskey and was headed back to get more when Sadie yelled, "Truth or Dare time!" I tripped over myself and caught onto the bar with both hands. I whipped my head around and stared at the little group. Really?

Chapter 16

It didn't matter that I'd tried to hide behind the bar, Stacy found me anyway, cup in hand. "Come on, Elly. It's your turn to get even with that bitch," she snickered in my ear as she pulled me back towards the group. "Elly wants to go first!"

My eyes were wide as I looked at the grinning faces. I shook my head, "Oh, no, I was just suggesting that we um, spin like a..." The alcohol was making my brain fuzzy and I struggled to find the word for the long glass thing that beers came in.

Kent, with his straight-laced self, came to the rescue, "Bottle?"

I pointed at him and nodded so hard I felt like I might fall over. "Yes! A bottle."

Sadie giggled, "I love that idea! Nerdy guy..." She was speaking to Kent, "Jen's boyfriend? Go get us an empty beer bottle."

He was tense again but he obliged. He disappeared for a minute before coming back with a bottle. He took stuff off the coffee table and put the bottle on its side in the center.

"I think Sadie should spin first," he said, calmly. I sat down on the floor across from Jen and Kent with Stacy by my side.

Sadie shrugged. "Okay! Rules are that if someone refuses a dare or a truth then they have to do the punishment that we, as a group, decide on." She spun and it pointed at the blonde guy. Sadie grinned.

"Truth or dare?" she asked.

"Dare," he said, without any consideration.

"I dare you to french kiss Jen!" She giggled as the blonde guy got up and crossed in front of Kent and kissed Jen. Jen seemed to be enjoying it. Kent, however, did not. His jaw twitched and his hands were balled up in his lap.

I almost felt bad for him as Jen fanned her face with her hand as the blonde guy sat back down, winking in her direction playfully.

"Right, my turn," he said with a chuckle. He spun the bottle and it landed on Stacy. He grinned at her, the pot had already solidified them as buddies. "Truth or dare, Red?"

She grinned at the nickname as she tossed her bright red hair over her shoulder. "Truth." She was a safe player, like I was.

"Who was the last guy you thought about fucking?"

I gulped. Okay. Maybe truth wasn't the safest way to go with this crowd. Stacy rolled her eyes, "Ummm...." She pointed at blondie and he grinned.

"Right on!"

It was my turn to roll my eyes. I drank a little more whiskey as I waited for it to get interesting. When Stacy spun it landed on Kent.

"Truth or Dare?" she asked of him.

He honestly looked like he wanted to kill someone, maybe himself. He took too long to answer and got a nudge in his ribs from Jen. "Wake up, babe."

His jaw flickered. "Dare."

Stacy flashed a shit-eating grin at me before declaring, "I dare you to spend seven minutes in heaven," she pointed to a tiny bedroom off in one corner, "alone. With..." She bit her lip and paused for anticipation purposes. I wanted to slap her for it. Who was she going to say? Herself? Jen? Sadie?! "Elly."

I blinked, stunned for the second time that evening.

His eyes shifted from Stacy, to the offending door and then to me. I felt shivers move through my body. Me?

He looked at Jen. "Alright."

Jen frowned at him briefly and then pasted on a smile, "You could always just decline, I'm sure the punishment wouldn't be as bad." Her hand moved to his wrist, gripping it.

I was still in shock. Me? I felt my cup tipping and I looked down to see Stacy's hand pushing it upwards. It had been dangerously close to spilling on the carpet.

My eyes moved back to Kent as he stood, and dislodged Jen's fingers from his wrist. "What are you worried about?" he asked as he moved towards me. I shrank back slightly. He wasn't really going to do it. Seven minutes alone with me? Before I knew what was happening he grabbed my cup and finished off the contents.

"But..." I tried to protest as he sat it down on the coffee table behind him and grabbed my hand, pulling me to a standing position. "But..." I glanced at Stacy and then at Kent. "But..."

My feet were moving but my brain wasn't the one making them do it. He pulled me into the dark room and shut the door behind us. I couldn't see him in the darkness but I could feel his warm hand around mine. I wondered what he was going to do to me. I wondered who he was going to pretend I was to get through it.

When he didn't make any moves I tried to break the tension, "This isn't exactly my idea of heaven." I heard his body moving but I couldn't see him. I tried to loosen our grip on each other but he held my hand tight. My eyes struggled to make anything out in the darkness but they failed.

A knock on the door behind me made me gasp and Stacy's voice filled the room, "Hey! You only have six more minutes left! We want to hear some noises or see some hickies! It's Seven Minutes in Heaven, not Seven Minutes of Quiet Time!"

It was as if that was all he needed to get into action. His hands rested on my hips and I could hear the smile in his voice, "Six minutes. Who is getting the hickey?"

Goosebumps rose on my flesh at his words and his closeness. I panicked and pushed him away. "Oh Kent...Oh yes! Oh my God, yes!" Kent didn't join in so I continued. I could drunkenly pretend to be getting some for six minutes if I needed to. "Yes, Kent! Lick it! Ohhh yes... just like that," my drunk mind really liked the sounds the pretend Kent was bringing out of me.

Jen's voice drifted through the door, they must've been just on the other side listening, "Pft. She's totally faking it."

So maybe I wasn't as believable as I'd imagined I was. "Push me up against the door," I whispered to Kent. He did so quickly, his strong hands grabbing my arms. He pulled me against him, our chests melded together. I held my breath and it left with with an "Oh!" as he pressed me against the door again with a thud.

I couldn't see him but I felt him, his body still pressed against mine. My heart was beating wildly in my chest and I was sure he could feel it too. "Do you like being bossed around in bed?" my voice was still just a whisper. The grunt that came from him spread through me, making me wet. I could feel his breath on my lips and smell the whiskey. "Push me against the wall again. Harder."

And he did. Either I had drowned out the noises on the other side of the door or there were none. I was lost in the seven minutes I had with Kent. "Oh, Kent... yes..." I'd meant it that time. Him taking control of me was blazing hot.

Jen's voice briefly cut through my thoughts, "Is she—" but it was cut off by the blasting of The Rolling Stone's "Beast of Burden." My adrenaline was pumping and I felt the need to do something crazy. I leaned forward and pressed my lips to his. Yes, he was with Jen. Yes, he'd been a dick and ruined my Christmas Eve earlier. But there was still some time to make this Christmas Eve not suck quite as bad. I wanted to kiss him to spite Jen. I wanted to kiss him for me. The spark ignited me and I felt his lips start to come to life as I slipped my fingers into Kent's hair.

That kiss was between us but I wanted to leave my mark on him, to make Stacy proud. I kissed my way to his neck and then latched on. I felt him pulling away so I tightened my grip in his hair to keep him still. His neck tasted of salt and he smelled faintly of something spicy. I focused on keeping the seal of my lips on his skin. He groaned and I eased up just a little. When I felt my lips give out under the pressure I pulled away. I wasn't sure what it was going to look like because I'd never done that before but I was hopeful that it would be huge and dark.

"Are you drunk?" I asked him softly. I wanted to know if he

was conscious and in his right mind.

"Bad...bad..." he replied.

I still couldn't tell if he was drunk or just slightly inebriated. "What?" I pulled back from his neck, and then remembered I couldn't see his face. It was pitch black.

"I told you not to drink and..." he snickered softly. All I wanted was for him to put his hands on me some more.

"And I did it anyway. Are you going to give me a spanking?" My head was fuzzy and I was vaguely aware of the saucy words that were coming from my mouth. His hands tightened on my hips. That was a good thing, wasn't it? I turned around in his grasp and put my hands on the door. I pressed backwards, my ass against his crotch. He was enjoying himself. "I was such a bitch to you, Kent. Do it. I deserve it. For everything I've done to you lately." Sleep sex included.

"Elly," he whispered my name and I felt my knees weaken. I could orgasm to him just whispering my name. There was a knock on the door.

"Time's up, you two!" There wasn't time before the door was pushed opened, throwing us both backwards. A slice of light hit Kent who held up his hand to block it from his slitted eyes.

I blinked at the brightness as it shone on him and smiled. "Is that a hickey?" the blonde guy asked.

"No, it's a fucking mole that you didn't notice before." I shook my head as I pushed past both dudes and made my way to Stacy. I put my arm around the back of her neck and squeezed, pulling her sideways with me as I sat back down on the carpet, "Oh my god. I could kill you right now."

She grinned and tried to pry my arm from around her neck. "Sounded like you should be thanking me."

"He didn't do anything. It was all me." Even to me my voice sounded laced with disappointment. Kent hadn't made any moves on me. He had been a perfect boyfriend. The only thing he'd done was get a boner and that was just his body responding to my female body.

"Elly! Wow! That's one hell of a hickey! Look at that, Jen!" Sadie covered her mouth with her hand as she stared as Kent made his way towards the couch where Jen was, a sour look on her pretty face.

Kent was grinning like he'd just lost his virginity to Linda Lovelace. "Yeah it is. Awesome job, Elly," Stacy piped in. She wasn't making fun of me and Kent looked relatively proud of himself so I let her go.

"You let her do that?" Jen asked.

"We kissed too," he said with a grin, bigger than the last.

She frowned and sat back, crossing her arms over her chest. "You got what you wanted, didn't you? How was it?" I'm pretty sure she was hoping he'd say it was disgusting. I was fully prepared for him to say that.

His brown eyes turned to me as he smiled. "Nice," he said, his voice was thick like honey. I blushed as I held his gaze.

"We have to go," Jen said abruptly.

"Jen, don't go! You didn't even get a turn yet." Sadie's voice did nothing to take away from the joy I felt. He said it was nice!

Kent's gaze left mine as he was pulled to the stairs by Jen, "Merry Christmas, everyone." She didn't sound like she'd really meant it. But I felt it. The compliment from Kent was an awesome Christmas present. And the only one I received from him that year.

Chapter 17

I was sitting by the window of the coffee shop, a well worn notebook on the table in front of me, a pencil in one hand, a steaming coffee cup in my other. I was finally completely over my breakup with Nate, or so I thought anyway. I'd written enough lyrics about the pain of rejection, of not feeling good enough. It was so emo it was making me sick.

So today I was trying something different. Trying to imagine I was with Kent, living happily ever after in the alternate universe that was taking place every night in my dreams ever since that night we'd shared a couple of months ago.

The words were flowing onto the page until a soft familiar voice spoke to at my side, "This seat taken?"

I would know his voice anywhere. My heart fluttered as I looked up and smiled, "Kent." I got up and wrapped my arms around him, forgetting that I was still trying to avoid him. Remembering why I had been keeping my distance as soon as I touched him. The sparks flew into my fingers, through my body and right between my legs. I pulled back and sat down, the blush on my cheeks evidence of my arousal.

"Um...no, please. Sit," I said. I motioned to the empty chair across from me and then quickly turned my notebook over since the lyrics I was writing were about him and his name was doodled all over the page.

"It's good to see you, Elly. You've been busy, huh?" That smile didn't move from his lips as he sat down across from me. His eyes moved to the notebook for a moment but they quickly went back to me. "How'd you do on the final?"

"Oh, um. I don't remember. I did okay, I think. Seems like so long ago. How about you? How did you do?" I sipped my coffee slowly, my attention solely on him. I wasn't going to tell him that I was so wrapped up in what had happened between us that I failed. I was going to be retaking that class over the summer.

Kent shook his head. "Got a ninety eight. I assume you did well. At least I hope so." He grinned. "It's been a while since I've seen you. I've been busy myself. I'm not sure what's been up with Jen, but she's been," he hesitated as he found the right word, "extra nice."

I nodded and smiled, though it didn't reach my eyes because the news partially saddened me. "Well, nice is good, isn't it?" I asked.

Kent shook his head. "It's...odd. She's just not herself. But whatever, I'm not here to talk about Jen. I'm here to talk about you."

I shrugged my shoulders, eyes still on him. "What about me?" Inside I perked up just a bit. Was he going to to dump her anyway to be with me? My heart fluttered more.

"How's the singing going?" Kent took a sip of his iced coffee, his eyes solely on me.

"It's good, yeah. Still doing open mic nights. And I'm writing a song for my independent study class. How's the geeking going? I heard there was a big gaming competition last month, did you go?"

He smiled and put the iced coffee down on the table. "Yeah, Jen signed me up for it, actually. I finished second overall. Got a new gaming system and three hundred dollars."

I nodded slowly, a real smile on my lips now. "Nice. Is that what you've been busy with? Gaming on your new system? What kind did you get? The Xbox or the GameCube?"

"I got the XBox. You've really got to come see some of these games, it's crazy how far they've come."

"Definitely, I mean, maybe when we're both not so busy. Finals are coming up quick and I know how busy your summers are."

"I'd like to hang out but yeah, we're both kind of busy right now."

"Are you guys going to the Hamptons for the summer again this year?" I sipped more of my coffee. Hoping against hope that he'd say no.

He nodded, staring at his cup. "Yeah. We weren't going to go but Jen's mom felt that she wanted to take us. Said something about making it a tradition."

My heart dropped to my knees. So he wasn't going to dump Jen for me. He was still happily in his Jen bubble. He was going to spend his summers in the same bed with her. He was going to chase her on the beach and hold her against him while the waves tried to take them out to sea. I tried to keep the disappointment off my face.

I lifted my shoulders as I inhaled deeply, trying to push the thoughts away and focus on the present, "So..." I exhaled softly and my shoulders dropped again, "I guess you're that guy who marries his high school sweetheart, huh?" I smiled softly, holding my coffee between two hands, holding back the immense pain at the thought. My alternate universe was extremely alternate. A fantasy of Star Trek proportions. He was quiet so I continued, "I mean...you two are still pretty serious, I don't really see an end in sight for you. She's being nice and you seem...happy."

He nodded, meeting my eyes. I saw something in them. Something that told me that his simple nod was not the whole truth.

My heart stuttered and I tried to calm it down at the thought that maybe there was still a chance for me, for us. "Right? I mean..." I broke our stare for a moment as I looked down at the table. "I know you didn't want to talk about Jen but..." I left it open, letting him have the start of that conversation if he wanted to take it.

"I mean, things shifted almost instantly when she got back from helping her mom move. She was nice, and I mean, not just to me. She asked me what I wanted to do, and who I wanted to go out with. She bought me lots of things. She's still buying me things. I guess it's her way of trying to fix things, but, I don't know what made her change all of a sudden."

"Huh. That's kind of weird." I searched his face as he stared at his coffee cup, twirling it slowly in his hand. My gaze moved to his hand and I was so distracted thinking about his hands, how they'd touched me. I swallowed hard and shifted in my chair. "Well, if I were you I wouldn't complain. Maybe she's just coming out of the funk from her parents' divorce."

He shrugged and gave a nod. "Yeah, maybe. She hasn't been drinking so much either. Thanks." He smiled at me and my insides churned.

"Anytime you need someone to try to rationalize women for you, just come find m—" Kent's cellphone interrupted me. I looked away, letting him answer.

He reached into his pocket to get it on the second ring. "Hello?" On the other side of the line Jen was talking. I couldn't make out what she was saying but I recognized the sound of her voice.

"Alright, I'll meet you at the house then. Bye." He hung up then slid the phone into his pocket. "I'm going to have to go. Jen says she needs to talk to me. Immediately."

I looked at him and nodded, "Of course. It was good to see you." I stayed in my seat, blinking back the disappointment. I only hoped he didn't recognize it.

"It was good to see you, Elly." The words that came from him were soft. He stood, waved and left me alone again at the table.

I watched him leave and wondered what was so important. I sighed and flipped my notebook open again. My final was in a couple of months and I didn't even have the lyrics nailed down, much less the melody.

Chapter 18

It had been weeks since I'd seen Kent at the coffee shop. Weeks of pouring over what he'd said to me. And what he hadn't said. Something in my gut told me that he had been waiting for me to admit to him that I was in love with him and that I wanted him to leave Jen behind and be with me. He hadn't said he'd wanted to be with Jen until death parted them.

I'd written song after song about him, about us, and about our future. It helped immensely to sort out my feelings. When I wasn't pouring over my notebook or plunking the piano keys in the music room, I was with Stacy. We'd grown closer and closer. I'd told her about that night with Kent and everything that had ever happened between us. She was the only one who knew how I truly felt about him.

But tonight was different. Tonight I was going to let everyone know about my feelings for him. The thought that he might be in the audience only excited me more. The music study final performance was a bi-annual event and generated much needed income for the music department. They spared no cost in advertising on campus and off.

I waited backstage for my turn and I was oddly calm. Usually I was buzzed before a performance. The adrenaline would take over and push me through, but not this time.

This time I felt sure. Absolutely sure. I hadn't felt so sure about anything in my whole life with the exception of choosing music as my major. I would perform my ode to Kent in front of everyone. And then when it was over I'd perform it privately for him. And beg him to do what was right. Beg him to choose me and give us a chance. Because I knew in my heart that we were meant to be together. Jen was just practice. And a placeholder.

I smiled and clapped from stage left as Bethy finished her violin composition.

"Great job," I whispered as she passed by me.

She squeezed my arm gently. "Good luck, Elly."

She kept walking and I turned my attention back to the stage. The lights dimmed and the spotlight moved to meet me. The crowd that had gathered for a couple hours of entertainment went silent. I inhaled deeply. Exhaled deeply. It was time.

I knew my mother was out there somewhere, probably holding up a video camera, so I had to make sure that it was perfect and inspiring. I sat down at the piano and positioned my hands over the keys. I leaned forward and spoke softly in the mic. "My name is Elly Palmer and this is my final composition of the year. It's titled "Plea.""

I sat back and the piano played the soft melody I'd painstakingly crafted over the past few weeks. Hours and hours of hard work played in the span of three minutes and fifty-three seconds.

My performance went off without a single hitch. The auditorium filled with applause as the last note reverberated through their eardrums. I waved as I left the stage and was met with Stacy when I was safely behind the curtains.

"Oh my god, Elly! That was beautiful! Do you think he was here?" She hugged me tightly and then pulled away.

I grinned at her and shrugged, "I don't know. It was supposed to be your job to look for him."

"I tried but it's so crowded out there."

"I know. I wasn't prepared for that many people. My knees feel like jello."

Stacy walked with me towards the chairs that had been set up backstage. "Well, take a breather. Did you want to grab a bite after this?" She sat down next to me, her hands clenched between her legs.

"Ah, no. I think I need to go find out if Kent was here," I said. Stacy grinned and then nodded. She looked so happy for me.

I hoped that look would be on Kent's face later after I sang him my song. Stacy jumped and pulled my phone from her jean pocket. She held it out to me.

"It's my mom," I smiled as I picked up the phone. "Hey mom."

"Hello, Elly. You were so good! I regret now that we didn't push you harder earlier in life."

I smiled to myself. She could've pushed but it wouldn't have helped any. "I would've ended up hating music and you. Listen, I need to go talk to Kent but I'll be home this weekend with all my stuff on your doorstep."

"Alright, dear. I'll be home waiting for you. I'll make sure you have clean sheets."

"Thanks, Mom. I love you."

"I love you too. Bye." My mother hung up the phone and I stood up, looking at Stacy as she joined me.

"Moment of truth..." I nibbled on my lower lip nervously.

Stacy grabbed my shoulders and gave me a little shake, "He'd be crazy not to say yes, Elly. You're amazing and I've seen it too. He does have feelings for you. You just have to get him to show it."

As I left the concert hall, I was filled with confidence and ready to confront Kent. I knocked on his dorm door, guitar case in hand. Jen answered and smiled brightly at me.

"Elly! Hey, how are you?" She slowly pushed her blonde hair

over her shoulder which I thought was weird.

"I'm good. Is Kent here?" I furrowed my brows and then tried to look behind her into the dorm.

"No, he's not. He went out for something for dinner. Our celebration dinner." She put her hand over her chest and that's when I saw the sparkling diamond ring. I blinked at the ring and felt the color rush from my face.

"I...uh, wow. You're?..."

Jen nodded enthusiastically. "Engaged! Can you believe it?!"

"That's...wow."

Jen closed the distance between us and hugged me. I let her because I was still very much in shock.

"I know! Isn't it exciting?!"

I felt like a dagger had been pushed through my heart and I was grateful that Jen couldn't see the hurt in my face because she was too busy hugging me. When she pulled back I grabbed her hand and pulled it close so I could look at the ring and hopefully avoid Jen catching my feelings.

"It's beautiful. Congrats."

Jen smiled and stared at her ring. "It's not very big but he got it from his mom. I'll be picking out the wedding ring myself and it's going to be so much prettier."

"I'm sure it will." I smiled softly, trying to push back the nauseous feeling. "Well, just...tell Kent I stopped by...or no, don't. Just tell him congrats for me."

Jen nodded. "I will. Bye Elly! Have a great summer."

"Yeah...you too." I turned and walked somberly down the hallway. The high from my awesome performance was now gone.

He was getting married. He had asked his mom for an engagement ring. And he hadn't told me. He had left me out of it all. I grabbed my phone and started scrolling through it. Had I missed some phone calls from him? Text messages? No. Nothing. I felt pain in the corners of my eyes and blinked as my vision blurred. My chest squeezed and I tried very hard to keep it together until I got to the privacy of my dorm room.

Later that night, I heard a soft knock on my door. I didn't know who would be knocking on my door at this late hour but if it was some weirdo wanting a booty call or something I wasn't interested so I yelled, "Wrong door! Go away!" My voice was scratchy and raw from the crying I'd been doing since I'd come back.

There was another knock. It seemed the person on the other side was either ignoring me, or didn't hear me.

I exhaled loudly and rushed to the door, opening it violently, ready to yell at whoever stood on the other side. My words froze in my throat as I saw Kent standing there. I saw his smile light up and then fade as he took in my appearance.

My mind was racing, I knew he could see my tear stained face, my puffy eyes. I stepped back so he could come in and looked down at my bare feet. A suitcase was on the bed, half packed, my walls empty, boxes packed and half packed all around the edge of the small room.

He stepped into the room and shut the door behind him. "Elly, what's wrong?" His eyes moved around the packed up room and stopped on the suitcase.

"Nate and I broke up." I lied, he still had no idea that we'd broken up months ago so it was time to get it out and save face because the real reason was too painful to admit. I wiped at my eyes and went to my dresser, continuing to pack.

"I'm sorry to hear that, Elly." He kind of stood there awkwardly.

"What's up? Are you here because Jen told you that I came by?"

"You came by? Jen didn't tell me anything about that."

I turned from the dresser, bras in my hands and stayed across the room from him. I smiled, hoping like hell that it looked sincere, "So congratulations are in order. You're getting married."

"Yeah, and I guess you heard the other news too, huh?" he asked.

I shook my head slowly. "What other news?"

Those dark eyes of his looked towards the floor. "Jen is pregnant."

My mouth dropped open. "But, I mean, that's not why you're marrying her."

"So, are you really upset about, Nate? Or is it something else?" He wasn't looking at me.

Why would he be asking me that? Did he come to my final? Did he hear my song? I wasn't going to ask him, not now that I knew he was marrying Jen, had been planning it long enough to find a ring for her finger.

"Don't be stupid, of course I'm upset over Nate. So tell me, is that the only reason you're marrying her?" I was looking right at him, but Kent still wasn't looking at me.

"I wanted to come tell you and hoped you would be happy."

"I'll be happy, but only if you are." I stayed across the room, not trusting myself to stop touching him if I started. "Are you happy?"

"I'm happy." The words sounded sure, but I swore there were tears in his eyes.

"Are you about to cry because of how happy you are?" I motioned to his eyes. My sappy tears were clearing up as my anger pushed through. Anger at him for lying to me. Anger at him for being so careless and knocking Jen up. He ruined everything! He always did.

Finally his eyes looked up at me and his tears seemed to be threatening to spill. "Why are you being so mean, Elly?"

"Because you're being stupid!" The dam was open and there was no closing it now. "You're repeating the history of your parents, don't you see that? Your dad knocked up your mom, didn't really love her and then left her high and dry when he couldn't take it anymore! You can't coast through life, Kent! At some point in your life you're going to have to stand up for yourself." I shook my head as I stalked over to my suitcase and threw my bras in.

Kent stood there for the longest time. The tears had already spilled from his eyes. He was never one for confrontation, ever. There was only that one time that he had a confrontation that I saw. At our first high school party a guy was picking on me and Kent punched him in the face.

His face became solemn as the emotion faded from his eyes. The tears still stained his cheeks as he turned away from me.

"I'm sorry you feel that way, Elly. I hope you have a good summer."

When he shut the door I reached for my stereo and turned it up loud, loud enough to cover the sobs that racked my body when he walked away from me. I felt, in my heart, that it was forever.

Chapter 19

Fall 2003 - Senior Year

I glanced around the packed bar, a smile on my glossy lips. A guy dressed like a cowboy wolf-whistled and put his arm around me as I tried to get to the bar. "Princess Leia, will you be my slave?" I laughed and held tightly onto the golden chain that was around my neck.

"Not tonight, cowboy." Luckily for me, the men had plenty of eye candy tonight and moved on quickly when I showed my disinterest.

I was almost to the bar when I tried to squeeze past a nurse and a maid.

"Elly!" The nurse's voice made me jump and look at the face. It was Jen, and holy shit for six months pregnant she looked very... unpregnant. "Who are you supposed to be? A belly dancer?"

There was a tall dark-haired person behind her wearing a lab coat who turned around after Jen spoke, his hands in his pockets. Kent looked as good as ever and it made me a little bitter to admit that. I had hoped that after our fight and our summer hiatus that he'd look like shit. He was wearing a lab coat with a nice polo under it, dress pants and shiny shoes. Around the neck of the lab coat was a stethoscope.

I cleared my throat as I met Kent's eyes with my own. "I bet Kent knows."

"Princess Leia, the Sex Slave, of course." Kent offered a little smile as he stood there but I didn't return it. "It looks good on you," he said. The comment got a nudge from Jen to his ribs.

I raised my hands in surrender. "I don't want to cause any premarital strife."

Jen gave me an unwelcome hug. "It's okay, Elly. I was just giving him a hard time."

Kent was standing behind her and raised his hand to scratch the back of his head with a chuckle.

I smiled softly and pat Jen uncomfortably and then pulled back, looking her over. "So you are due in what? Three months?"

Jen looked over her shoulder at Kent and shook her head, "No. No, I lost the baby over the summer."

I nodded slowly and looked from Jen's face to her hand and then to Kent and saw that the ring was still there. I looked at Jen.

"I'm sorry to hear that. I can't imagine how tough that must have been." It was the only genuine thing I'd said to her since we started talking.

Jen nodded again and reached out, gently clasping my elbow. "We missed you at Kent's birthday this year!" She looked over her shoulder at Kent. "Why didn't we invite Elly?"

I didn't need to hear whatever lame ass excuse they had for "accidentally" misplacing my invite. I wouldn't have gone anyway. It took me all summer but I had finally come to terms with the end of my relationship with Kent. And I didn't need to stand there and pretend that I wanted to be friendly to either of them.

"Must've slipped your minds. Sounds like you had a hectic summer," I said. I pointed to the bar sheepishly, "I'm gonna go get my drink. I'll see you guys around." I raised my hand and waved at them both before turning away, heading for the bar to order myself a shot.

I was glad to be away from that train wreck of a relationship. I didn't need him in my life anymore. Once my tequila shot arrived I tilted my head back. I blew out hard trying to calm the fire as it slid down my throat. I looked at the clock and then around the bar, smiling softly as I took in all the costumes. The girls, much like myself, dressed like a bunch of sluts. The guys costumes ranged from super lazy to super crazy.

Someone dressed as Chewbacca came up next to me and put a hand on my boob and honked it. I looked over my shoulder and laughed, slapping the hand away.

"Want a drink?" I asked.

Chewie nodded and then pulled off her mask. It was a girl. Man-ish in a tall way but certainly not a man. I ordered another shot and then pushed it to my bandmate, Susie.

I watched her take the shot and then looked around the bar again, my eyes meeting with Kent's. He was standing at the other end of the bar, a beer in one hand, a Cosmo in the other. He stared at me and seemed torn. He stuck his tongue out at me.

Susie's paw waved in front of my face and I turned away, breaking the spell.

"Earth to Elly! It's time, girlfriend."

I nodded and then looked for Kent again. When I spotted him I stared for a few seconds and then moved away, Chewie following. More Star Wars characters were on the stage, tuning their instruments and that was where I was headed.

I made my way up on stage and grabbed the mic. I cleared my throat and started speaking, "Happy Halloween!! We're the Duds..."

I looked behind me at the band I'd joined over the summer. We were all a bunch of self-proclaimed nerds and had an awesome time playing and spending time together. They saw me through my heartbreak with Kent since Stacy was not around. They allowed me to musically unleash my feelings. I looked at the drummer and nodded my head. The music started, No Doubt's "Don't Speak" filled the bar.

The men in the bar cat-called when I bent over to get a drink of water as the intro played. I looked behind me and grinned, moving a slow hand up my bare, toned, shimmery leg.

I looked out into the crowd as the words poured from me, I

couldn't see past the bright lights but I knew he was out there and yes, damn straight, I was singing this with him in my heart and soul.

The last of the chorus was sung with everything I had. I felt like I was on fire whenever I was on stage, it was where I was meant to be. The applause was deafening and we continued right into our next song, Blur's "Song 2." The bar was a collective "Woo-hoo!" when the song called for it and the pulse was live through the jumping, dancing crowd. After the short two minute Blur the Kent-smashing continued with Alanis's "You Oughta Know." I touched myself during the interlude, touched myself on my shoulder where he'd kissed me the night we'd had sex and then it got more intense as I matched the lyrics with a scratch on Chewie's back. I went through the set list as it alternated between a crowd-pleaser and a Kent-killer.

They lowered the lights for the last song, the spotlight off of me. The soft guitar intro of "Lips of An Angel" drifted through the bar. My eyes searched the crowd and landed on Kent who stood there at the bar, his eyes on already on me. He had two drinks in his hands again but didn't move while I sang to him.

I closed my eyes at the end of the song and then spoke into the mic, "We're the Duds! Thanks for coming out tonight!" I gave one wave and then turned off the mic, the applause overpowering anything I would've said anyway.

I made my way to the bar, pushing through the crowd. I ended up at Kent's side and ordered myself another shot of tequila. I glanced at him but wasn't going to say anything to him unless he said something first. Kent sat the drinks down and pulled some money out to pay for my drink.

"I'm sorry, Elly."

I pushed his money back to him. "I get free drinks on gig nights."

Kent took the money and put it back into his pocket. "I was listening to those songs and the words. I know some of those were meant for me, Elly."

"And you're apologizing because...?" I stared up to him, not letting him get away with being vague tonight.

Kent looked like he was having trouble finding his words. "For how we left each other before summer. "

"Oh. You mean how you just walked away from me?" My eyebrows lifted in unison along with my voice.

"Yes. For how I left you. I know you were crying as I walked out of your dorm room. That's what I was sorry for."

I threw back the shot and set it gently on the bar as I swallowed.

"No apology needed. I'm good. Singing is very therapeutic. I hope you two are happy together." I reached up and put my hand on his cheek, my thumb grazing at the very corner of his mouth gently. I knew I was playing with fire but I just couldn't seem to help myself. But being friends again wasn't in the cards.

His face turned just slightly as if he were going to kiss my thumb. It was much like the way he kissed my cheek that night we'd slept together.

I was pulled to the side abruptly, my hand leaving his face. "Stop flirting, Princess," a male voice purred in my ear.

The man who held me had blonde spiky hair, multiple face piercings, and a mean look about him. He was dressed like a pimp complete with the tall feather in his hat. I smiled at him and wrapped my arms around his neck and stepped close, pressing myself against him. I wanted to be sure that Kent got an eyeful. I wanted him to regret his choice. The choice he continued to make. The wrong choice.

"Make me," I purred back. He flashed me his charming smile which kicked his looks up at least four pegs. He pressed his lips to the side of my exposed neck.

"Gladly," he growled in his deep, raspy voice. I giggled and looked in Kent's direction. Kent was picking the drinks up and was getting ready to move back through the crowd.

I smiled, I bet it stung on the other side of the table. I knew, I'd been there. Before Kent could retreat all the way Jen came by and tapped me on my shoulder. I turned around and was met with the sharp sting of Jen's open palm. My head whipped to the side and my hand covered my cheek. There were collective gasps and "Ooh"s in the immediate area. I turned my face, hand still on my cheek and glared at Jen.

The crackling of glass breaking sounded in the background as Kent moved up between us. He seemed angry. Very angry.

My boyfriend put his arm around my chest, holding me back.

Jen looked at Kent and then pointed a finger at me. "She was groping you!"

Kent looked at me and then looked at Jen. "Let's go, now." He grabbed her by her upper arm and pulled her through the crowd.

I still had my hand on my cheek. "Bitch." I fell back against my new boyfriend and turned, heading to an empty booth with his hand on my hip, not looking back. Good riddance to both of them.

Chapter 20

Kent had only tried to contact me a few times after the bar incident. One of them was on Thanksgiving. He hadn't left a voicemail so I didn't feel obligated to call him back.

I didn't want to see him or Jen at Christmas so I skipped it and let my mom know I'd be coming in after the party was over.

As I walking up the driveway I saw Kent standing outside in the cold. His cheeks were rosy with color and so was his nose. His hands were tucked into the pockets of his thick jacket. I froze when I saw him and then turned on my heel, heading back down the sidewalk.

My heart hammered in my chest as I heard him call out my name. I heard his footsteps as he came jogging up behind me. "Elly, wait." His hand wrapped around my arm to stop me. I yanked my arm away and turned around, my voice thick with anger.

"What?!"

"I'm sorry. I blew up because of Jen's jealousy issues. She got in the way of our friendship."

"Newsflash: That's what she does! And she'll continue to do it because you're getting married to her. You know, I was glad she slapped me. I deserved it. I did. But I won't give her a reason to do it again. I'm staying the hell away from you." I tried to step around him but his large hand stopped me.

"Elly. I've talked to her about it, a lot. Either she accepts the fact that we are friends or it's over between us. I'm not willing to lose you, Elly. I'm sorry."

I pulled my arm away again. "You've already lost me, Kent! Just accept it like you do everything else."

"No, Elly. I will not accept that. We've been through some hard times together and I'm not willing to give up."

"I have nothing to give you. What we had...It's gone. We can't hang out anymore. Our lives are rapidly going in different directions."

"Will you take a ride with me? I have a gift for you, but it's not here."

"No. I won't accept any gifts from you." I tried to step around him one last time.

Kent stepped in front of me, his hands up in defense. "At eight years old we made a promise to each other, that we'd be friends forever, no matter what. I intend to keep that promise and that is what this gift is about. It's something that goes with that promise."

"Yeah, but we aren't. So, you broke the promise. You broke it when you started dating Jen and let her come between us. You broke it when you walked out on me last year and didn't call me all friggin' summer."

"Then what am I doing here now, Elly?"

"You're trying to take it back but you can't." Tears pricked at my eyes and I struggled to keep them from falling. "Tell me this Kent, if I said that in order to get me back as a friend you'd have to break off your engagement to Jen and never talk to her again, would you do it?"

He reached into his pocket and pulled out his cellphone. "I'm not going to lose you, Elly." His fingers started typing in a number, I could only guess it was Jen's. "Is that what you want me to do? Is that what all this is about?"

I stared at him and shook my head, looking down at my feet. I wasn't going to force him out of his relationship. Even if he wasn't with Jen there was no guarantee that he'd pick me and then we'd be in the same situation just with a different girl. "No, I'm sorry."

"I stood up for myself with her. I told her that you were going to be my friend and she had to stop being jealous. I came here tonight to say I was sorry." He put his phone away and got down on his knees in front of me, his arms limp at his sides, like a man defeated. "I'm begging. Do you want me to crawl? Because I will." He bent forward, putting his hands on the ground too.

"Kent..." I stepped away from him, "Stop. Is this what you did for her too? Crawl on your hands and knees? Beg her to stop being jealous over me?"

"No," he sat back on his haunches, "she begged me. I told her how things had to be or we weren't going to work out. Then I told her that I was going to be friends with you and that I had to show you I was sorry. I also told her that I wanted to get a gift for the both of us. She wasn't happy, but it was accepted. So will you take a ride with me? At least come to my car so I can show you what I want to do?"

My curiosity got the best of me and I felt my wall going down.

"Reluctantly. I will." I waited for him to stand up and lead the way. I followed him to his car slowly. Feeling...I had no idea what I was feeling.

I looked over my shoulder at my mom's house, the lights were all off and I swore I saw the blinds move upstairs. I huffed softly, my mom still had her hopes up that our friendship would be repaired obviously. And she'd been the one to tip Kent off that I was coming home. I'd have to talk to her about that later.

When we got to the SUV, which was parked a few houses down, he opened the door on the passenger side. There was a stack of papers in the seat that he was filtering through. He pulled out a design and held it out to me.

"It's a symbol for friendship. There's a tattoo parlor downtown that's open tonight."

I laughed and shook my head, "Wait. What? You want to buy me a tattoo?"

He waited for my laughter to stop, staring at me in the dim street light with a serious expression on his feet. "I want to buy us a tattoo. I've wanted one for a long time but I was picky about what I would get. Now I've found something I'm willing to put on my body for the rest of my life. Are you?"

I wrapped my arms around myself and shrugged. "I don't know. You're going first. If you cry then I can't do it."

"I'll go first and then I'll be right there with you." Finally, a little smile appeared his lips. "So you'll take a ride with me?"

I nodded slowly. Part of me felt that this was a terrible, terrible idea. Another part of me had been missing him terribly and was desperate for any little crumbs of attention he'd give to me. "Yes, but I'm not promising anything else."

"Fair enough."

Chapter 21

He picked up the pile of papers in the passenger seat and threw them in the back. He moved around to the other side and got in. Kent started the SUV and turned the heat on to try and warm it up. He was shivering. I reached back and grabbed the papers before buckling up. I flipped through them while he drove. There were several other things doodled on paper. One of them was actually a rather well done drawing of me.

I looked at the drawing, held it up to my face so I could see it better in the darkness. "Who drew this?"

"Remember Sammy from Art History class?" He was watching the road as he drove. "He drew all those for me."

"Does Sammy have a crush on me?"

"That was a possible tattoo I was thinking about. I gave him some pictures of you to draw."

"Hmm." I kept flipping as I mulled that over. Jen probably twisted his arm and told him he definitely couldn't get a picture of my face on his body. I smirked as I imagined them having sex and her having to stare at me on his chest. I shook the thought the away, amusing as it was.

There was also one of my name ornately drawn out and his name mixed into it. Another of two video game controllers, with tangled wires.

I laughed at that one. "You do love your video games."

"It was something we always used to do, not about the video games themselves." He pulled into the tattoo parlor.

I flipped to the one we were going to get, or maybe just him, I hadn't decided yet. "Where are you going to get it?"

"Diamond Thief. It's the only parlor that is open at this time and I've looked at some of the work. It's good." He put the car in park and looked at the parlor in front of us.

I laughed. "No, I meant where on your skin."

"If you can't tell I'm kind of nervous," he chuckled as he looked at the sign that flashed with the large diamond on it. "I was thinking on my arm, maybe my calf."

"I think it should go on your hairy ass." I grinned at my own joke, surprised by how easily I could slip back into being his carefree friend.

Kent smirked. "Is that really where you think it should go?"

"Will you put it there?"

"Do you want me to put it there?" He chuckled as he opened the door and got out.

"It's your body..." I got out of the SUV too and walked with him up to the door of the tattoo parlor.

"Where do you think it'll look good?" He opened the door for me and we were greeted when we walked in by a girl sitting behind the desk. She had lots of colorful tattoos on her arms and facial piercings.

"I don't know. I haven't seen your body lately."

"You've seen my body, it hasn't changed since the last time I came out of the shower or the that time I mooned you in the kitchen."

I was uncomfortable thinking about his body so I blurted out the least sexy place I could think of. "Your wrist."

"Alright." He moved up to the girl, who smiled sweetly at him. "Yeah. I need a tattoo done. Maybe two." He turned his head to look at me. "She still hasn't decided yet."

The girl nodded her head. "Can I get a copy of the thing you want?" Kent took the slip of paper I was holding and gave it to her. She stood up and disappeared into the back of the shop. She returned in a few minutes with the picture. "Where do you want it and how big?"

Kent held wrist out to her. "Big enough for the wrist." The girl nodded and disappeared again.

I looked at Kent, smiling. "You're really doing this. Where should I put mine?"

Kent leaned his elbow on the desk as he waited for the girl to come back, his boots crossed at his ankles. "So you're going to get it? I say your chest." His eyes moved to my buttoned up coat and then shook his head, his eyes meeting mine. "I'm just kidding. How about your hip? Or a little farther over where there's more meat so it doesn't hurt so much?"

I smiled. "Maybe I should get it on my wrist, too. Or maybe on my lower back. I've always wanted a tramp stamp. Ooh! How about on the bottom of my foot?"

Kent made a face. "That sounds painful." He chuckled. "I like the wrist idea then we'll match."

"Okay. Let's do it."

The receptionist came back out and looked at me. "How about you, darling?"

"One of the same, hon."

"Alright, just let me see your wrist." When I offered it she took it and measured it with her finger. "I've got one artist tonight so it'll have to be one at a time. I'll get you set up, beautiful. You want to take your man back to the chair?"

"He's not my man..." I pointed at the drawing, a little panic in my voice. "Does that symbol mean he's my man?"

"Oh. I just assumed. I have no idea what the symbol means, sugar." The girl was cute in an emo way because of the black hair and tattoos. "Anyway, I'll get Matt out here in a minute when I get the sheet set up."

"Is Matt hot?" I smiled sweetly.

The girl looked at Kent and gave a little grin. "He kind of looks like him, 'cept with lots of tattoos and glasses."

"Mmm...glasses." I looked at Kent with a grin. "Sounds sexy." I looked back to the tat lady. "Is he single?"

She looked me over slowly, starting at my feet and when her eyes met mine, she said, "We do couples, if you're interested."

Kent snickered and moved for the tattoo chair.

I blushed and then shook my head. "Oh, no...no, I'm pretty vanilla...sorry..." I didn't follow them. "Blood and stuff, I can't." I sat down in the waiting area and picked up a magazine.

"You know where we are if you change your mind." The tat lady winked at me and took a seat behind the desk again. The guy Matt came out of the back and surprisingly he did look like Kent in a way. The old Kent.

Soon I heard the needle start up and watched what I could see from the waiting room which was Kent's non-tattoo arm and his leg. They were resting casually. He didn't grunt or squeeze the arm of the chair too tightly. I wanted to get up and have a look but I was afraid of the blood.

About an hour and ten magazines later Kent stood from the chair. "Not too bad," he said as he examined it.

I couldn't wait to get this over with so I bolted back there and sat down in the chair before the warmth disappeared. "My turn!"

Kent grinned down at me. "Want me to hang out? Or you want me to wait over there?"

"Here, just don't let me see your bloody wrist." I closed my eyes and turned my head away from his raw wrist.

Kent chuckled as he looked at the artist. "Can your girlfriend wrap it up for me?"

Matt looked up at Kent. "Yeah, the wife can take care of you. I'll wait on ya before I start on your girl."

I looked over and watched as Kent started out of the room and then stopped. "She's not my girl."

Matt's beautiful eyes raked over my body. I felt warmth pool in my belly. "Shame."

Kent pretended he didn't hear it and went to get his wrist wrapped up.

When Matt put the tracing on my arm I screamed and jumped. He grinned at me, "Sorry, doll. I didn't start yet...relax..."

I nodded slowly. "I'm trying..." It wasn't as easy as he made it sound.

Kent returned with a bandaged wrist and took a chair, pulling it over next to me. "The needle hasn't even started yet! Come on. Give me your hand."

"Maybe Matt should hold my hand. He reminds me of high school you, back when you were nice and geeky." I stared at Matt, fascinated.

Kent smirked as Matt laughed. "You're a mess, doll." Matt started the needle up.

I squealed and shut my eyes tight. "Oh my god!"

I felt an arm around my shoulder and assumed it was Kent's. "I got you, Elly. Just look at me. Open your eyes and look at me and think about things from the past. Anything that doesn't deal with right now."

The panic rose inside of me as I heard the needle draw closer to me, "I can't...Kent, I can't." I pulled my arm back from Matt and put it against my chest protectively. "I need booze, lots of booze. Please! ...Or a roofie?" I looked between the two guys who looked like they could be brothers.

The needle gun turned off. "You give me some extra cash we can work somethin' out." Matt said as he stood up. He went to the window and turned the "Open" sign off.

I looked at Kent and nodded my head. "Give him some extra cash!"

Kent reached into his pocket hesitantly and pulled some money out. "How much, man?"

Matt looked between us slowly. "Forty bucks and I'll toss in some booze and shot glasses."

I pouted. "I was hoping for the roofie."

"That's eighty bucks, doll." Matt winked at me.

I slapped Kent's chest. "Give him the eighty bucks!"

"A roofie? Really, Elly?" Kent sighed but pulled eighty bucks out and handed it over to Matt.

"Alright. You guys stay right here and I'll be back in a minute."

I looked at Kent and smiled. "My first tattoo and my first roofie, all in the same night. This is the best Christmas present ever."

I could hear Kent's soft laughter behind me. After a few minutes of waiting Matt returned with a glass and offered it to me. "It's a shot, but you'll be out of it in about ten minutes. You won't remember a thing."

I pointed at the both of them. "Don't get any ideas. And tell that to your wife, too." I downed the shot and then sat back, smiling.

"The wife got a little interested when I snuck to the back, but she told me you already said no. Your loss, doll." Matt grinned, sitting on his stool, waiting for the drug to kick in.

"Merry Christmas, Elly." Kent was chuckling softly as he looked over my face.

"Thanks. Merry Christmas to you too." I inhaled and exhaled slowly, focusing my eyes on Matt. It was easier to talk to him somehow. "I drank like two six-packs on your birthday. And then I puked all over my bathroom."

"I drank almost a fifth of rum by myself and blacked out."

"What? Where was Jen?"

"With the people at the party."

"You weren't at your party?" I put my hands down at my sides and closed my eyes.

"No, I was there. But you weren't, and I was depressed. So I drank, a lot. I threw up on Jen."

I smiled, eyes still closed. "That would've been awesome to see. Kent..." it was getting harder to talk, my brain grew hazier by the second, "that night...I can't forget about that night..."

"Which night?"

I couldn't respond, the roofie had fully kicked in and I was out like a light.

Chapter 22

Things were kind of fuzzy for me, but I was starting to come around. I was on my back and under covers, it seemed like my head was on a pillow. It was kind of dark in the room I was in. I was pretty sure it was a dream.

I moaned softly, "Kent?" I tried to open my eyes but they were still really heavy.

I felt someone take my hand. "Elly. I'm here."

"Kent..." I moaned softly as I took his hand and put it over my breast. It was my dream after all.

"Elly, you're still out of it." His voice was soft.

"Like you were. We'll be even and I won't remember, just like you." I weakly squeezed his hand under mine.

"Elly." He sighed and I felt the bed dip behind me as he almost spooned me.

I groaned softly and pulled his hand down away from my body, my eyes still closed, my speech slightly slurred. "I know...you don't love me that way. You never will."

He whispered my name, "Elly."

"Kent, I'll be a good friend from now on. I promise."

"I love you, Elly. More than you'll ever know. More than you'll remember." He sighed as his hand came up to stroke my hair slowly.

I moaned softly. I felt him slide closer and felt his arm move around my waist as he held me.

I turned over and snuggled against his neck and then kissed him there. My hand moved up to his cheek and I stroked it lightly. "Can't you just sleep with me one more time for pity's sake? Roofie sex is supposed to be good, right?"

I felt the muscles of his jaw tighten and loosen under my hand. "Elly, I .. " His voice faded away.

My hands went up into his hair, running through it slowly, much the opposite of when he did it to himself. "One pity lay? I'm pretty much begging."

"I..." I felt his hand slid under me and his strong arm pulled me closer to him until our chests were pressed together. "All I want to do is feel myself deep inside you. I want to taste your lips and feel your skin against mine," he whispered.

I moaned and gripped the hair at the back of his head tightly. His dirty words making me wet. "Then do it. It will be our little roofie secret..." I was close enough now to breathe the same air as him and I inched forward until our lips touched.

When our lips met, the kiss from Kent was hungry, surprising my dreaming self. But a few seconds later the kiss was broken and I heard him take in a ragged breath. "Elly, this is.. rape. You're not in control of your body."

I whimpered and rolled away from him, "Even my sex dreams suck these days."

"You were of your own mind that night."

"Oh, so in this dream you do remember that night. It's turning around."

"I was awake most of the way through it. I remember it, Elly. All

I wanted to do was whisper your name."

There was some shouting on the other side of the door a few seconds before I heard it burst open. "You can't just burst in here, Jen!" My mom's voice called out.

"Kent! I'm not supposed to be jealous of this?!"

I groaned my eyes still closed, "And it just got bad again."

I felt Kent roll away from me, "This isn't what it looks like, Jen. Jesus Christ."

"No? It looks like you have a hard on in Elly's bed!"

"Oh god, Jen. I tried, okay? I tried to seduce him but he said no. Now go away so he can—"

Jen's voice broke through my zen, "So you can what? And what the hell is wrong with her? Is she drunk?"

"She was saying go away so I can leave and go home, Jen. Elly has had a rough night and I was trying to comfort her. She's had a lot to drink and doesn't feel good."

I started to laugh. "He roofied me. Kent paid eighty bucks for a roofie."

I heard my mom grumble, "Oh lord, Kent. Wait 'til I tell your mother."

Kent sighed in frustration. "Her Christmas present was a tattoo and she said she couldn't go through with it. Jesus Christ." I felt him moving the bed behind me. "We got matching tattoos."

"Whatever. Can we go now? She's in her bed and delusional anyway she won't remember a thing."

"Yeah, yeah." I felt the bed move again and then go still, as he stood up. "Goodnight, Elly. Merry Christmas."

I scoffed, "Would've been merrier without Jen in my dream."

I heard my mom yelling, "Kent, a roofie??" And then everything went black again.

Chapter 23

My wrist was on fire, my head was pounding. What the hell was going on? I groaned as I rolled over, trying to get comfortable in my bed. I hoped it was my bed. I couldn't remember anything after sitting down in the tattoo chair.

I groaned again. I got a tattoo. Kent made me get a tattoo. And whether I liked it or not I'd always have to think about him whenever I looked the underside of my wrist. He was good. Either I would think fondly of him for the rest of my life or I'd be seventy five and cussing his name as I stared at an old, wrinkly tattoo.

I wondered what we'd be like at seventy-five. Would we even still know each other? Would we live close? Would we talk on the phone or do puzzles together in the same nursing home?

Home... oh god, I hope he got home alright. I picked up my phone and texted him.

ME: IT HURTS!

KENT: UGH. MINE TOO.

ME: WHAT THE HELL HAPPENED LAST NIGHT?

KENT: YOU LOST YOUR TATTOO VIRGINITY?

ME: DID I BLEED ON YOU?

KENT: NOT ME.

ME: MYSELF?

KENT: NO. MATT, YES.

ME: WAS I BRAVE?

KENT: ...ROOFIE? YOU DON'T REMEMBER A THING, DO YOU?

ME: OH, RIGHT...AND AFTER THAT?

I waited for a minute or two and when no response came I forced myself out of bed. I had to pee really bad. When I came back I saw he'd responded.

KENT: JEN IS ANGRY BECAUSE SHE FOUND US IN BED TOGETHER.

In bed together?? I had a dream that we were in bed together. It was a very vivid dream. Did he? Did that happen? Was it not a dream? I typed my next question carefully, I didn't want to give anything away if it wasn't true. I felt my heart squeeze tightly in my chest and held my breath as a I waited for a response. If it was true then he wasn't sleeping when we, you know, did it.

ME: WHOSE BED WERE WE IN AND WHY WERE WE IN IT TOGETHER?

KENT: YOURS. YOU WERE OUT OF IT. CONFUSED. I WAS COMFORTING YOU.

Comforting me... okay. That was like the dream. Now for a test.

ME: DID YOU GRIND ON MY ASS OR WAS THAT JUST A DREAM?

KENT: I TOUCHED YOUR BOOB.

ME: WHAT??

KENT: YOU PUT MY HAND THERE. THEN JEN CAME IN AND YOU TOLD HER TO LEAVE.

Ohmygod, ohmygod, it wasn't a dream. All of that shit had really happened. And he'd confessed. He'd confessed to me. Why wasn't he mentioning that part? My scalp was tingling with anticipation. Maybe he was going to leave her. I stared at the tattoo on my wrist with a grin.

ME: AND YOU TOLD ME YOU WANTED TO SAY MY NAME THAT

NIGHT?

KENT: WHAT ARE YOU TALKING ABOUT?

My heart sank. I must have just imagined that part of it. I was a total skank last night. I made him grope me and Jen found us like that. How was I ever going to show my face around her again? Stacy shot me a text while I figured out what to say to Kent, reminding me that I was singing tonight. Perfect. I'd distract him so he wouldn't have to know about my crazy dreams.

ME: NOTHING. WHAT ARE YOU DOING TONIGHT?

KENT: YOU? XD

KENT: NOTHING.

ME: FUNNY.

KENT: SERIOUSLY. WHAT'S UP?

ME: I'M SINGING TONIGHT. U WANT TO COME?

A little square picture popped up on my screen. I squinted and recognized a half naked Kent holding his thumb up in the air. I chuckled. What a dork.

KENT: HOW'S THAT FOR AN ANSWER?

ME: ...IS THAT JEN'S BOOB?

KENT: NO, PERVERT.

Another picture arrived of a cream colored stuffed bunny. What the hell was he doing with a stuffed bunny in his bed? Maybe he was in Jen's. I couldn't think about that. He was engaged, for God's sake! I stared at the tattoo again. And obviously my friend.

ME: IS THAT A STUFFED SEX DOLL? WHO'S THE PERVERT NOW?

KENT: BAH.

ME: 8 @ CRAVE. CU THERE, PERV.

KENT: SURE THING, ROCKSTAR.

I texted Stacy back to let her know that Kent was coming

tonight.

STACY: I'LL BELIEVE IT WHEN I SEE IT.

Yeah, me too.

Chapter 24

"Will you stop it, please?" Stacy asked, her hand on my knee which was bouncing nervously.

I stopped the bouncing. "Sorry."

"If he said he's coming then he's coming, don't worry."

"Pft." I blew out a breath, "I'm not worried." I could act as nonchalant as I wanted to, but Stacy was my best friend and she could see through my bullshit.

She smirked. "Uh-huh."

"Whatever. I'm not." I checked my phone. How could it still be 8:05? I frowned at the phone, something was wrong with this thing. If Kent was going to be late he would've called. And he was never late.

What if he got into a car accident? What if something happened to Jen or his mom or something? What if Jen found out and wouldn't let him come?

I chewed nervously on my lower lip as I waited. It was going to be my turn any minute. I looked at my phone once more and Stacy put her hand over mine. She had a look of disapproval on her face. I sighed. She was right. I needed to chill out or I was going to have a panic attack in front of everyone.

I set the phone face down on the table and inhaled deeply, trying to get soothing energy into my body to replace the nervous kind.

"Next up is a veteran to our stage, Elly Palmer. Give it up." There were polite claps from the crowd as I grabbed my guitar and headed up there. I felt a squeeze on my elbow from Stacy.

"Go get 'em, girl!" She winked as I smiled and stepped up onto the tiny stage.

I took a seat and felt the familiar weight of the guitar on my lap. I cleared my throat as I looked around the small space. This was one of the few places open in our small college town on the eve of Christmas Day. It was packed with students who hadn't returned home for the break and other locals who just needed to get away from family for a couple of hours.

Still no sign of Kent. I felt the knots twist in my gut and tried to block out the disappointment that was starting to crush me. "I um," nervous laughter left me, "Merry Christmas everyone."

My fingers strummed the guitar softly, setting up a slow tempo. I took one more look amongst the crowd. I hoped against hope that he would have magically shown up. Just as I was about to drop my eyes back to my guitar I saw him. My heart fluttered and I momentarily forgot the words I was going to sing. My fingers knew the accompaniment, there were at least some small graces. I looked back to my fingers. Focus, Elly. I inhaled deeply and let "Hallelujah" flow from my body, slowly.

I didn't think about anything but the lyrics, the chords, the music for a blissful four minutes. The chords came to a close and applause erupted from the crowd. I grinned and looked out at their smiling faces, their looks of approval and felt my heart swell.

"Thank you," I said softly as I turned my gaze to Kent who was grinning in the front row, almost at my feet. "This next one is dedicated to an old friend of mine."

I turned my attention back to my guitar as I strummed the opening riffs of Kent's favorite bands, "3 Libras" by A Perfect Circle. I chose it because it fit my life. I made sure it was slow, angsty, so the crowd could feel the pain and desire that came from every word.

Again more applause met me as I ended the song. I held up my hand in thanks and stepped off the stage, guitar in hand. I made a beeline for the door before the post-crowd panic attack set in. I inhaled deeply as soon as I got outside. The door clicked closed and then opened again, the cacophony of the coffee house growing louder for a moment.

I looked over my shoulder and saw Kent, "I was hoping you weren't leaving."

I smiled softly. "No, not yet. I just need a minute. Could you get me a coffee?"

He hesitated as his eyes took me in but then he nodded and left me alone again. I wrapped my arms around myself when he left and took deep cleansing breaths. The cold air felt so good on my skin, in my throat and lungs.

He had come. I smiled as I remembered the look on his face as he admired me from below. It had only taken a year and a half but finally he had come. I'd half expected him to bring Jen with him too and I felt guilty for being glad that she wasn't here.

I stepped back into the building and shivered as the warm air met my cool skin. I coughed as I slipped through the tables towards the barista at the back. Kent and Stacy seemed to be talking intently about something and I approached I heard Kent say, "I want to talk to her about some things."

"Talk to me about what?" I asked as I stepped between Stacy and Kent. She held out the coffee and I took it with a smile. "Thanks."

"You bet. I'll be right back." She ducked between us and headed for the bathroom.

Weird. I sipped my coffee and stared at Kent who was looking at Stacy as if she were his life raft.

"So?"

"Jen wants the wedding moved up. To New Year's Eve. I told her that I wanted you as my best woman. But..."

Of course there was a but. But I wasn't pretty enough to be in Jen's wedding? Or Jen was too insecure in her relationship with Kent to have me stand beside him? Not that I could blame her, I was totally in love with him. I stared down into my coffee. Where the hell had that come from? Oh hell. I thought I was over him?

"She wants a traditional wedding. Which would require a male to be my best man."

I nodded as I took a sip of my coffee. I didn't understand why this was something he needed to talk to me about. Unless he was getting to a different point. "Uh-huh," I said, looking up, hoping he would continue.

"...I still want you to be my best woman. But I don't want to upset her. I want to support her. I don't really give two craps about the wedding so long as my mom and my friends are there."

"New Year's Eve, that's like less than a week away." Way to state the obvious, Elly. I cleared my throat as I looked down at my coffee, hoping it would magically get me out of there. "Just get some men for your side and I'll be your secret best man. Woman. Whatever."

When I dared to look back up at him I found him grinning again. "Really?"

I shrugged, "Yeah, it's not a big deal." I gasped in surprise as he hugged me, his long, warm, strong arms around my body made me feel so small, safe. My heart warmed itself up a few notches.

"It's a huge deal to me. Let me buy you some beers."

God, he felt so good, and he smelled so good. Did he say something about beer? Or did he call me dear? I opened my mouth to ask but he pulled away. Stacy was standing there, smiling expectantly.

"So?" she asked. "Did he tell you?"

"Uh-um..." My brain was drawing a blank, still busy playing Kent's hug in a loop.

He laughed beside me, "Yeah, I told her. And I'm buying you both some beers to celebrate Elly's acceptance as my best man."

Her eyebrows shot up as she looked at me. I shrugged. What could I say to her, really? That I wasn't really a best man, just a best man in secret? Everything really good between us since Jen had come along had been a secret.

"Well, you two have fun, I should probably get home and get some rest."

I felt my eyes about pop out of my head and I made a little motion with my head to try to get her to take it back. How was she supposed to get the signal when she wasn't even looking at me?

"Kent, we'll meet you outside in a minute." I handed Kent my guitar and then pushed him towards the exit.

He laughed as he stumbled. "Alright, Elly, geez."

I turned back to Stacy who wore a look of confusion. "What's the matter?"

"Are you kidding?" I glanced over my shoulder to be sure that he was gone. He was. Thank god. I turned back to Stacy and frowned, "If you leave me and Kent alone while under the influence of alcohol bad things are going to happen! Remember last Christmas? He kissed me!"

Stacy looked around and so I did too. People were staring so I guessed I was being a little too loud. I softened it down and put my hand on her shoulder, "Please? Please don't go yet," I begged.

She sighed and shrugged my hand off. "Fine. But if you two start making out I'm leaving."

I held my hand up in defense. No way was that happening. He was getting married in less than a week. I felt my stomach clench.

In less than a week he was going to be married.

Chapter 25

After the beers arrived Stacy wasted no time in starting the conversation, "You were so awesome. What was that second song though? Did you write that? I've never heard it before."

I sipped my beer to give myself a moment to breathe. I was having beers with Kent, like we were actual adult friends. He was sitting across from me and he looked delicious in a dark blue sweater. I couldn't get overexcited though because he'd just asked me to be in his wedding. Or a part of his wedding. He was getting married.

Remember that, Elly! He is getting married!

"It's a song from Kent's favorite band, A Perfect Circle. He's in loooooove with them."

He had talked about them so much in Art History class last year. He would hum their songs anytime he walked from one place to another. It was cute for him to be so into a band. Normally he would hum the theme song to whatever video game he was currently into. At least that's what I remembered from high school.

"Yeah, yeah," Kent smiled. "That's the best rendition I've heard. It gave me tingles."

I rolled my eyes, not accepting his compliment. He was just being nice. He probably hated that I'd taken the song and molded into something else. I didn't want anyone else gushing about me. What could we talk about that would change the subject? Sex? No. God, no. What was wrong with me?

"So...you need to find your best men. Did Jen throw suggestions at you?"

I jumped in my seat as Stacy's shouted and pointed at me. "That guy! She probably picked that guy we saw her with that time we were walking to the campus pool. Remember him?" She started to laugh and I laughed briefly along with her, my eyes looking over at Kent. Did he understand that we saw something uncool going on? He just sipped his beer. No, apparently he didn't.

"Yeah, I remember."

"God, I wanted to bang that guy. He was so hot," Stacy continued, lost in the her memory of 'that guy.'

I shifted in my seat, if she kept talking she'd get the the unsavory part. I smiled at Kent, "They guy must be in Jen's circle of friends. They were all hanging out together on the quad playing Frisbee."

Kent nodded and shrugged his shoulders as he moved back to the original line of questioning, "Well, there's Mike."

His old roommate, I nodded, waiting for him to continue but Stacy moaned beside me. I glanced at her, her eyes staring at the ceiling. I didn't want her doing something crazy so I nudged her with my shoulder, "Hey! Snap out of it!"

She grinned at me. "Sorry. He was some Latino goodness. Unforgettable."

I shook my head and looked back at Kent. "Mike and who else?"

Kent shrugged. "Paul, I guess? He was the jackass who beat me in the gaming competition last year. He's also a friend of Mike's."

"And why would you want the jackass to be one of your groomsmen?" Stacy asked, finally coming back to reality.

"While Kent may call him a jackass he has a deep respect for any man or woman who can beat him in a fair gaming competition." I wondered if that was why he'd picked Jen. Aside from being pretty and popular she had somehow managed to kick his ass at any video game she'd played with him. She'd played to bond with him and get his attention but she wasn't really into them. Her plan had worked.

Too well. I swallowed my jealousy down with my beer as Kent nodded his agreement to my statement.

Stacy turned to me, "So, are you going to Jen's bachelorette party?"

I looked at Kent, wondering what he'd want me to say. "Ummm..."

"Elly is taking care of something. She'll be busy with it until the wedding." Well that made me sound like I was going to be sewing her dress by hand. That was not the impression I wanted to leave with Stacy. I was no one's bitch. Mostly.

"What he means is that I wasn't invited. So, no, I won't be going."

"I see," Stacy laughed as Kent kept his head down, eating pretzels. He couldn't have respond without spitting them everywhere. Her attention was quickly drawn to a tall rocker-looking-dude who had entered the bar. "Hellooooo, stranger."

I grinned as I quickly looked him over. He had long dark hair, a tattoo peeking from under his collar and his ass looked extremely nice in his dark jeans. "He's doable," I said.

Kent looked too as I pushed Stacy away. She was rubbing up on me like I was that rock god she was drooling over, "Oh my god! I'm not him. You're so gross," I laughed.

"I'm sorry," she said, "I just..."

"Go get his number."

She shook her head, "No way. Guys like to chase the girl, don't they, Kent? Come on back me up here. Every guy loves a little mystery, don't they?"

I rolled my eyes, "Seriously?? He's never had to chase a girl. He's getting married in a week and he didn't have to chase her anywhere. She chased him. So obviously that's what guys want. Get your hot ass off the stool and go over there."

"She's right. I've never had to chase."

I nodded and looked back to Stacy who was biting her lower lip as she stared at the mystery man.

After a few moments she pushed herself away from the table, "Alright, I'll do it."

As Stacy sauntered off, Kent stood up too. "Want another beer,

Els?"

"Yeah, sure." I watched as Stacy flirted and then turned my attention to Kent who came back with the beers.

"So..." he tried to liven the conversation again.

"Mrs. Jennifer Lytle..."

"Sounds different, that's for sure." He nodded.

"It...does." I nodded back. It sounded wrong. It should be Mrs. Elly Lytle. Forever. Til death do us part. I looked away guilty. How could I stare at him and share a beer with him in his happiness at my acceptance of secretly standing by his marriage when my thoughts were solely on possessing him. It wasn't too late. He wasn't married yet. He would be within a week and then I'd miss my chance. What was I talking about? He knew how I felt about him, didn't he? He knew that I wanted nothing more than for him to dump her and proclaim his undying love for me. Kent cleared his throat, pulling me from my thoughts.

"Thanks for doing this, Elly."

"Doing what? Staring at you like an idiot? Sure, no sweat."

"No. For being my best woman."

I raised my eyebrows, "I mean... it's not like I'll be standing up there with you, holding your hand. But I'll make sure those guys are where they are supposed to be, if Jen or her mother or the wedding planner don't do it first. I'm assuming she has one, because, well, it's Jen. Oh my god, she's going to be such a Bridezilla. I'm so glad I won't be around her before the wedding."

"Yeah," Kent interrupted my verbal diarrhea, "I just want to get the tux on and fitted and then not have to deal with it. She wants everything to be perfect."

"I mean, obviously. She picked you." Before I knew that I had said it out loud Kent was speaking and I didn't have a chance to take it back.

"You're making me blush, Els."

Damage control time. Avert the conversation. Redirect it, quick!

Stacy came to the rescue. "So, his name is Rio. And I totally just gave him your number." I was mid-gulp on my beer and was not prepared for the news. I turned away and started to cough as I felt the burning of beer in my throat. I frowned at her but she kept grinning, "He's looking for a new singer for his band. And I said you were awesome and I gave him your number." She wiggled into her seat, "And he gave me his. And we're going to chill sometime."

I glanced at Kent. He was just watching and drinking his beer. I didn't want to be the only one feeling embarrassment or discomfort at the table. I liked to share the wealth. "Damn," I said as I turned my attention back to Rio, "He is hot. And in a band. Are you sure you're interested?"

Stacy smacked my arm and glared at me. "Yes!" She recovered quickly and continued to verbally drool, "His voice is like...oh my god. So deep and gravelly. It's so sexy."

"It's not fair that you always call dibs on the boys first."

"It's not my fault that you're too shy to talk to the boys."

She had a point but I wasn't going to admit to it. "I am not."

"Pft," She looked at Kent. "Have you ever seen her go up to a strange guy and just start talking to him?"

"She never has when she's been out with me."

"Well, I mean that's because—" I nudged Stacy with my elbow to shut her up.

Kent looked uncomfortable. Half my mission was accomplished. "Yeah, so..."

"Because Elly used to be fat and shy," Stacy blurted out. Although everyone at the table already knew I'd been fat and shy. I put my hand on my forehead as I ducked my head.

"Elly, prove her wrong. Walk over to..." I glanced up in time to see him scanning the bar and point to an attractive guy with long hair, "that guy."

Seriously? Kent wanted me to go hit on a guy in front of him. I felt the familiar squeeze of disappointment in my chest. "No. I don't need to prove anything to either of you."

"Good. Then dance with me before we call it a night." He finished off his beer and stood up, looking at me expectantly, his hand held out.

I shook my head. "No one else is dancing." I wasn't going to dance with him while everyone was staring at me, especially not Stacy. She'd probably record it on her phone and taunt me with it.

"Because no one fed the jukebox any money. No music equals no dancing," he said.

"Only one way to rectify that then, huh?"

"You promise to dance if other people are out there dancing too?"

"Sure," I retorted.

He grinned as he moved over to the jukebox. He stood there for a moment, mulling over the music. Stacy was watching him too as she finished up her beer. He stuffed some money into it and soon a few songs started to play. He stopped to talk to some people at the bar before coming back to the table. Just before he reached us a few couples moved onto the dance floor.

"He really wants to dance with you," Stacy chuckled.

"I don't know why," I grumbled softly just as Kent approached the table and sat back down. I waited and waited for him to ask me again. He just stared at the bodies on the tiny dance floor while the song played through. I sighed softly and finished off my beer. It figured that Kent would make a big fuss out of wanting to dance with me and then chicken out. It was the story of our lives.

Stacy giggled beside me, her eyes turned down to her phone as she busily texted. Just before the song ended Kent reached over the table and took my hand. It freaked me out a little bit, his touch was so warm and soft. And unexpected.

"Can I have that dance now?" he asked with a warm smile. There was something else there. Something that scared me and made my insides joyful.

He held my hand as he pulled me to the outer edge of the dancers. As soon as we stopped the song ended. I felt his hand slipping from mine, felt the disappointment in my gut. "Dammit..." His fingertips were on mine when he grabbed my hand tightly and pulled me against his chest. "Oh, wait a second. I wonder who played this song."

I rolled my eyes, trying to hide the excitement that I felt having his arms around me. "Please. I'm not a five-year-old. I know that you picked this song." I put my hands on his shoulders, ready to slow dance awkwardly middle school style.

He chuckled, I felt the vibration from his chest. "Always master of the obvious." My cheeks flushed as his hands went to my hips and pulled me even closer. "I really did want to say thank you."

"Got it, weirdo." Weirdo was what he was. Dancing with me like... like we were more than just friends.

"I'm serious," he said softly. His right hand ran up my back slowly, leaving a trail of tingles in its wake. His chin touched my temple and I was close enough to smell my favorite cologne on his skin. Did he buy it just to wear it tonight? Was it a gift from Jen he'd gotten for Christmas? I felt myself go rigid in his arms.

"So, since when did you change colognes?"

"I wanted you to say yes tonight. I'm not pulling any punches."

"...Say yes to what?" Was he trying to seduce me? Was he holding me this close and smelling so good so that I'd hop into bed with him?

"Being the best woman," he said.

I relaxed a little and tried to hide my frown in his shoulder. Stupid, Elly, stupid. Of course he wasn't trying to seduce you.

"Sure thing," I said softly as I tried to pull away, my composure back. He didn't let me, his hand pressed on my lower back, holding me in place.

"Relax. I just want to dance with you. Hold you close. I'm not going to try and kiss you or anything else."

I felt myself stiffen. I hadn't been thinking that, until now. "Stop bossing me around."

He grinned. "My apologies."

My mind started to wander as we continued to sway together. I wondered how many times he'd danced like this with Jen. I'd never seen him do it. Not even at prom. I shivered as I remembered prom. What a disaster that was.

"Since when have you liked to dance?" I asked, trying to distract myself from the fact that his hand was slowly moving down my back.

"Since I forced you into my arms," he said softly.

I felt my cheeks blush as I looked into his dark, glittering eyes. With his hands on me it was starting to wear on me. My mind was going places it shouldn't go. I dropped my gaze to his shirt.

"Um...so it grew on you?"

"Sure."

"Like ticks."

"No, more like..." he paused to think and pulled away.

"Cancer?"

"No," he grinned at me.

"That ugly dog poster your aunt got you for Christmas?"

He chuckled, "No, like that snowman sweater your mom insisted was adorable."

"The haircut you thought was super cool."

"Oh, god no." His nose wrinkled in disgust, his lips curling with amusement.

"Or me bossing you around."

"Yeah. You bossy person." His smile faded a little from his lips, but it was still there in his eyes.

I realized in that moment that the time between us being close friends was probably going away. I wasn't going to get to boss him around. That would be Jen's job. I felt my heart sinking and I pulled away before I couldn't hide the hurt. "Thanks for the dance. I just remembered I have to go plan a bachelor party."

"Yeah, you have a lot of work to do to make it an epic party."

"No, it's going to be low key and nerdy. Like you." I said, poking him in his chest. His hand caught mine and I felt my cheeks flush. I was saved by a strong hand pulling me backwards.

Chapter 26

"Soo, I've been texting and Rio wants to play pool," Stacy said as she stepped between me and Kent.

I rubbed my shoulder. Damn, Stacy was strong. "O...kay, that's great. Have fun?"

Stacy stepped to the side and grinned between us both, her hands twisting her phone slowly, this was not going to end well. "He wants to play with us. Us against you two."

"Um..." I looked at Kent, silently asking him if he wanted to do it.

"I'm game to kick some ass." He was so confident. So falsely confident. He'd never played pool with me before. I sucked, but I didn't want to burst his bubble.

"Ok! We'll do it."

Stacy squealed and bounced. "Yay!"

As we set up the game it was revealed that this was no ordinary pool game. This was like beer pong, but with pool table pockets and pool balls instead. The boys flipped a coin and Kent won. He nodded at me, I was up first.

I cleared my throat, bent over the table and put my stick into position. I looked like I knew what I was doing but I was awful. I missed the balls in the middle of the table twice but whacked them softly on the third try, causing the balls to scatter mere centimeters from each other on the outer edge. I bit my lower lip as I glanced around. Stacy and Rio were grinning. Kent looked shocked at my lack of skills. But when he looked at me he smiled and shrugged.

I moved over to him slowly. "Sorry," I whispered. When I looked up Stacy had sunk two striped balls into corner pockets.

She pointed to us and then to the shots already on a large tray on the table. "Drink up, bitches." Rio gave her a high five and then lined up to take his turn as we both downed two shots each.

"Don't worry, Els. We can still make a comeback."

It turned out that we couldn't. Six shots later we were groaning and more than a little toasted. I had a feeling she'd done this on purpose and I didn't appreciate it. I pointed at Stacy and Rio and yelled loudly, "You. Guys. SUCK!" My finger swayed just a bit even though I willed it to remain still so I could look as serious as possible.

"Don't be jealous of our skills." Stacy grinned as she wrapped her arm around Rio's waist.

He looked down at her. "They gonna need a ride home?"

She shook her head, "No. Elly is taking a class and has her dorm just down the street. Kent can go too. Or call his fiancé."

Rio glanced between us and shook his head. What the hell was his problem? Never seen a boy and a girl be friends before? Or had he caught me staring at Kent's ass earlier? Oh god. The room was tipping.

Kent's arm went around my shoulder and pulled me towards the pool table. "Come on, I'm going to show you a thing or two before I throw up all over the place."

Stacy had yelled something about leaving but I was too distracted because Kent had bent me over the pool table and his arms were around mine. "Trying to teach me anything is pointless. Especially after eight shots." I stilled my hips when I realized I was wiggling my ass against his crotch. Not that he'd seemed affected.

"Act like you're going to shoot at one."

"This is cheating," I said. He was all but holding the stick with my hands.

"This isn't cheating. This is how you play pool, silly," his breath warmed my ear.

"It's not how I play pool."

"You handle a stick well, at least," he said.

"I do not. You are helping me handle my stick."

He laughed. "This all sounds so dirty."

"I wish it were dirtier," I murmured. I felt his lips on my neck and gasped, "Kent," I whispered.

His hand left the pool cue and came to rest on my hip. Another kiss touched my neck. Fire was collecting in my belly as I gasped again. His other hand moved to my hip. He pulled me back and spun me around to face him.

I somehow managed to pant out his name, "Kent?" What was he doing? Why? What? I searched his face, he didn't look nearly as drunk as I felt.

"Your lips numb?" he asked so softly; it was barely audible.

"Probably," I whispered back. I fought back a moan as my nipples grazed against his chest.

He pulled me in closer and pressed his lips to mine, hard, as if he were laying claim on them. I kept my hands on the table, I didn't trust myself not to strip his clothes off in the middle of the bar.

He pulled away and stared at me for a long moment. I didn't say anything, afraid that if I said something it would break whatever spell he was under. He took me by the hand and pulled us both through the side door that led to the alleyway and the cold winter air.

My body stiffened against the frigid air and my mind was starting to clear. What the hell was he doing? Was he going to kill me now? Oh my god, I was losing it. "Kent?"

My mind fogged again after he pushed me against the hard brick wall and kissed me.

"Dorm?" he asked as he pulled away, his thumbs stroking my hipbones. I nodded and pressed my lips to his again. I wanted more, I wanted all of him. I wanted to feel him inside me again. He put his hands on my cheeks and held me in place as he pulled away.

"Need..." his lips came back to mine for a second before they pulled away again, "your stuff."

I pulled back and stared at him. What did he say? My stuff? He was thinking about my stuff at a moment like this? Why was he even able to think clearly? "I..." Where was my stuff? "It's in the bar."

He pulled me off the wall only to push me back up against it, kissing me hungrily before he pulled me back into the bar.

I followed after him, a huge smile on my lips. It was happening. My fingers were interlaced with his and as soon as we were inside I pulled on his hands. I laughed as I almost fell into him. I pushed him against the nearest wall and kissed him again, my lips would never get enough. And my hand found the front of his pants. I wanted that. That was going to be mine.

"Say my name, Kent," I whispered against his lips.

His hand closed around mine and squeezed, stilling it. He pulled back, his eyes were tightly shut, "Elly, I can't..." He sighed heavily, "This..."

I pulled away quickly and the contact we'd shared, the intimacy was gone. What was I doing? Had I forced him into this again? Had I tricked him...again? "Oh, god." I dropped my gaze, my hands on my head. "I'm so sorry. I'm terrible. I..." my hands moved through my hair as I turned away from him and started the seemingly long walk back to my stuff.

His fingers were around my wrist when I grabbed my purse. "Elly, hey. We've both had a lot to drink. It's not a big deal."

I gathered all my strength and smiled at him, "Yeah, not a big deal. Totally. Thanks for coming to see me sing tonight." I grabbed my stuff and then hugged him tightly. I bit my lip to keep my sobs in. Soon I could let them out but not just yet. Not in front of him. "Okay, I gotta go." I kissed his cheek, probably for the last time, and let him go. I grabbed my guitar and got the hell out of there.

Chapter 27

Two days before the wedding I arranged for Kent's bachelor party. I took being the undercover best man very seriously. I planned everything and paid for it all too. I wanted to make it the best since I'd all but raped him a few nights ago. I owed him at least this much.

The limo parked in front of Kent's mom's house and honked to draw him outside. The music, bass heavy rap, was vibrating the limo and the surrounding houses. I was with the other two groomsmen, all of us with our top halves sticking out of the top of the limo, beers in hand.

Kent had no idea. And it showed on his face when he opened the front door and eyeballed the limo. A neighbor came out on her porch to see what the noise was. "Sorry, Mrs. Sharp! I guess it's my bachelor party since I'm getting married in a few days. When they bring me back I'll make sure the music is down!" Kent called to the neighbor lady as he ran out to the limo and climbed in.

"Wooo!!!! KENT! KENT! KENT!!" We were cheering for him and disappeared into the limo when it started to pull away from the curb.

I grabbed a beer and opened it, holding it out to Kent. "For you, Bachelor!"

Mike, Kent's freshman roommate turned good friend, shared Kent's love of video games and they spent lots of time trying to best each other that first year of college. He sat back and lifted his bottle. "You lucky bastard. Jen is one sexy lady. And a tiger in the bed, I hear.

Whew."

Kent blushed as he took the beer and held it up. "Thanks, guys. I had no idea. This was a pleasant surprise."

Mike grinned. "The surprises are just beginning."

I rolled my eyes at Mike. "Don't give it away, dude."

Kent raised his eyebrow and looked around the limo with a smile before he turned the beer up.

I was dressed up for the occasion in a black pencil dress, the skirt ending just above the knee. My hair was curled loosely, a red flower in my hair to match the red piping that accentuated my tiny waist. I sat back after raising my beer with Kent and took a sip, pressing my knees together to keep from flashing everyone.

Mike was dressed in a light blue button down shirt and black slacks. The other guy, Paul, was the guy who kicked Kent's ass in the gaming competition. He was more on the heavy set side, he spent a lot of time in front of the console. He was dressed in a gray button down and dark jeans. His dirty blonde hair was slicked back and his beard was trimmed back neatly.

We rode around for twenty minutes, entering the outskirts of the city. My tattoo had healed enough that it was no longer bandaged and on display to the world. It flashed Kent as I lifted my hands up and danced in my seat to the loud music still thumping the leather seats.

We stopped in front of a building lit up with lots of red and pink neon. "Pussycat Palace" flashed through the window.

Mike grinned as he leaned over me to look out the window. "Yes!"

I pushed Mike back with a grin. "Too close to the goods, man!"

Kent's curiosity was piqued and he too sunk down in his seat as he tipped back his beer, emptying it.

The limo driver opened the door so we could all climbed out. I was first, followed by Mike. Paul motioned for Kent to get out and followed after him. I stood at the front, the pink and red neon casting a glow on the guys' faces.

Kent looked up at the sign and then his eyes fell on me a little grin on his face.

I grabbed his hand and pulled him up to the entrance. "Come on, dammit, we have a lot to do tonight!"

"Fine! I'm kind of scared to know what you guys have planned."

Paul and Mike flanked us. I let go of Kent's hand once we stepped into the strip club. It was dark, the stage was at the very back of the large space and it was illuminated by lots of hot lights. A thin large-breasted stripper was already in her thong shaking her booty for the money that paid her bills. The smell of sex and stale beer was heavy in the air.

"Me too." Mike mumbled and then stumbled to the front of the strip club. "Have you ever been to strip club before, man?"

Kent shook his head at Mike. "Never have been, no. Guess that's why I'm scared." He laughed nervously.

A waitress dressed scantily with cat ears approached us with a tray on her hand. "You guys have a seat at an empty table and I'll be right with you." I nodded and then leaned in to say something in private to the waitress. The waitress assessed the three guys and then looked back to me, nodding. I punched all the guys on their arms and then led the way to a dirty table that was right in front of the stage.

A waitress came by after we sat down and bent over, her breasts popping out from the top of her bra. I couldn't help but stare along with the boys as they moved rhythmically with the wiping of her hand. When the waitress stood up straight she smiled at the boys. Mike cleared his throat, his hand went under the table and he pulled out a five dollar bill and held it up. "Damn baby, that was...damn."

Paul and I laughed loudly. I looked on stage, the song was over and the stripper was crawling on the stage, picking up the thrown bills. I looked away quickly, naked girls were definitely not my thing.

I noticed Kent's avoidance matched my own and I nudged him and pulled his head down to me so I could speak into his ear. "Kent, it's your last chance to stare at a woman's boobs. What's the problem?"

I saw his eyes move towards the stripper as she stood up on stage and moved off of it. Kent moved his head to whisper in my ear. His breath tickled it slightly sending shivers through me. "This is normally something I do alone, looking at naked girls."

I glanced at Mike and Paul, who had no shame ogling the breasts that were all around them. I pulled back, my hand on his chin so he couldn't look away from my eyes. "Kent. No one is watching you. Don't be a lousy bachelor or I'll embarrass you." I raised my eyebrows to question if he understood what I meant.

The waitress came back and set the shots down on the table. I nudged Kent and pointed to my seat which was right in front of the stage. "Switch with me!"

He shrugged his shoulders and then swapped with me. I pushed the shots around and then toasted with them. The MC took the stage and announced that it was time for amateur strip night to begin.

Mike and Paul looked around and hooted. The MC called the ladies to come to the stage so they could register. I stood up after most of the girls went up and followed, making a face of surprise at Kent from above him.

I watched as he looked at Mike and at Paul in disbelief but when he looked back up at me I saw a little smile move across his lips.

I wasn't the best looking woman on the stage, certainly not the one with the biggest boobs but Kent was probably only going to be single for another few days and I had to show off while I still could. It would be something we could keep secret between us for the rest of their lives at the very least. Another one. I winked at them as I waited. After I was registered I went backstage with the rest of the girls.

There were lots of girls. Lots of hot girls. Girls who knew how to dance, girls who knew how to twirl on a pole and girls who didn't need to know either of those because their bodies were smoking hot.

Mine was the last name on the list and I'd picked an Aerosmith didy. The first few riffs of "Crazy" played as I stepped on stage dressed in an oversized men's white work shirt and black boy shorts. The waitress had made sure to hook me up with something strippable but not gaudy as requested earlier.

I wasn't the best dancer but I wasn't laughable either. It wasn't until the first chorus that I grabbed the pole and started to twirl around it. I didn't do anything spectacular just yet. I was still warming up. I took off my shirt, unbuttoning it slowly to reveal a black bra. I threw my shirt at Mike who hollered his appreciation, which caused me to grin.

I noticed that Kent's eyes seemed glued to me as I danced, a smile on his lips.

I turned around and slowly pulled the boy shorts down, stepping out of them slowly for effect. I stood on stage revealing my itty bitty black g-string. I laid down on the floor, did some teasing leg lifts and moved back to the pole.

People were whooping for me and I heard Kent give me a cat call whistle, the one that was unique to him. I'd only ever heard it when we used to watch Tomb Raider. It was, regrettably, more than once.

Practically naked, I started climbing the pole. I wrapped my legs around it when I reached the top. I bent backwards, hanging on just by my creamy thighs. I grabbed on with my hands and then lifted my body, gyrating on it a couple of times, imitating sex.

They cut me off at three minutes my last moves were of me spinning around the pole. Once I was done I went to the middle of the stage and did a bow. I grabbed the boy shorts and waved, a blush on my cheeks. As this was not the performing I was used to, not on stage anyway. Many of the pounds I'd shed had been done on a pole.

All the girls returned to the stage and I tried to hide behind the other girls, my arms crossed over my chest. "And second runner up is Candy!" Candy jumped up and down, showing off her huge, natural boobs. My eyes were on Kent, making sure he was watching the big boobs flopping all around, I knew it was his thing, but he still had his eyes on me, grinning. I shook my head at him. I made a throat slitting motion and then pointed at him.

"First runner up is a fan favorite, not her first amateur night, Jessi!" Jessi was the best dancer of the group by far. I clapped politely not that it would've matter because there was more than enough noise for her.

"And tonight's winner..."

"Elly!" I jumped when someone pushed me forward, I bit my tongue and covered my mouth with my hands. My eyes were wide with disbelief.

I accepted the check and then bowed again as "Crazy" played over the speakers.

Kent was waiting for me to come back out and as soon as I was within reach he picked me up, and spun me around. "Oh my god Elly, that was...Wow!"

I squealed and pushed against Kent's shoulders. "Oh my god! Put me down!" I laughed. Mike and Paul were waiting at Kent's side.

He put me down, grinning from ear to ear. "By the way, Elly. That was hawt."

"Oh my god. Knock it off." I slapped him playfully on his stomach. "This is what's hot." I waved the check in front of my face. "One thousand big ones!! Should cover the cost of this shindig."

"After talking to Mike, I know who made the plans here. What else do you have up your sleeve Ms. Palmer?" Kent held his hand on his stomach from the slap.

"You'll just have to see." I winked at Kent and didn't protest when Mike put his arm around me, his hand low on my hip. The two of us led Kent and Paul out of the club. Mike's hand was on my bottom, pushing her into the limo gently. "More shots!" He called out as he took a seat next to me, his hand on my knee, possessively.

I abandoned my spot on the seat for a minute as I went to the little compartment next to Kent. I pulled out little bottles of Jack and was about to hand one to Kent when the limo stopped suddenly.

I fell backwards, my quick scream filling the limo. Mike reached out and tried to save me but he was tipsy and his arms weren't quite there. I landed on my back, half on Mike's lap, half on the floor. I looked up at him and he looked down at me, grinning. "That's a good look for you."

Paul snatched his bottle from my hand while I was close.

I laughed, "Don't be a creeper, Mike. You're supposed to be hitting on the strippers, n...I mean the real strippers."

"Looked pretty real to me."

"Whatever." I put a Jack in his now empty lap and then went back to Kent, sitting next to him. I put a tiny bottle in his hand and then opened mine and held it up to him. "To your last boys night."

He smiled softly and lifted it to mine, the little plastic bottle necks tapping together. "Yeah."

The guys opened their bottles and held them up in a toast. "Hey-yo!"

Chapter 28

The next stop was at a dark public park. I grinned. "Hope you boys are ready to play."

Kent slammed the bottle back and took down the contents. He made a face and breathed out as he tried not to cough because of the alcohol. He looked outside the window and saw blackness. "What?"

"Get out. I need to change real quick." I grabbed my bag and waited for them to leave. Paul got out first, followed by Mike hesitantly.

"We've seen it all already." Mike got out and closed the door, leaving me and Kent alone.

Kent paused at the door, his hand on the handle. "What you did tonight, Elly. It was amazing."

"I've been practicing, it wasn't so great." I smiled softly.

I looked down at my bag in my lap and started unzipping it. "Before you go can you unzip me?" I slipped my shoes off quickly and then turned around, my back to him.

I felt his hands come to the dress, his knuckles were warm, his fingers shaking just a little. "No. It was really good, Elly. I couldn't take my eyes off of you."

"It was dark and the light was on me there wasn't anything else to see." I pulled my hair to the side.

His fingers took hold of the zipper and slowly, almost

painstakingly, lowered it as he spoke. "No. You were awesome. It wasn't because there was nothing else to look at."

"Are you drunk too?" I laughed softly and looked at him over my shoulder.

"Not yet. I'm still in control of my mental functions." He paused at the bottom of the zipper.

"Then you need to drink more." I stood up, but bent over because it was short in the limo. My ass inadvertently in his face.

I quickly pulled on a pair of tight black spandex pants. Followed by my sneakers and a fuzzy hot pink pullover. "Ready to get your ass kicked?" I opened the door to the limo and pushed him out.

The limo driver went around to the trunk and opened it. Inside were four light sabers.

I looked around at the men. "What the hell are you waiting for? Grab your lighted dick stick and let's go! The winner gets a super special prize." I reached in and grabbed the pink one and then stepped back in a defensive stance.

Mike, intrigued by the idea of a special prize, grabbed his next. Followed by Paul.

Kent took the last one, which ended up being purple. "I feel like Mace Windu from Star Wars," he chuckled as he twirled the lightsaber.

I grinned as all three of the men started twirling their lighted futuristic swords. "Alright. You have to be gentle on the girl. But boy on boy you can hit as hard as you want as long as it's not the face. And go!" Immediately Paul and Mike went for Kent, chasing after him.

"What the hell is this? Double teaming?" Kent was fast and ran circles around them as he laughed. He took pop shots at them when he could. He ran figure eights and tried to get them close to me. I wasn't going to miss my chance.

I ran up behind Mike and stabbed him between his arm and side. "Gotcha! You're dead, dammit."

Mike faked his death and dropped to the ground, gasping. "Damn you, Elly...," his dying words.

Paul was on Kent, he was a hardcore gamer and not taking it

easy on Kent in this situation either. He liked to win.

Kent pushed right back at him just as hard. "Remember I said I feel like Mace Windu?" Him and Paul thwacked each others swords. "That's also Samuel L. Jackson, which means I'm a bad motherfucker!" Kent knocked Paul's sword away and hit him across the chest.

Paul cursed and then put his hands up showing he was done. Paul and Mike leaned against the limo to watch the showdown.

I held my pink lightsaber up and smiled behind it.

Kent faced me, a smile on his face too. "Alright, Elly. What you going to do? Hmm? You going to come at me or am I coming at you?"

I grinned back. "You think I'm going to tell you my secret plan of attack?" I slowly circled with him.

The purple lightsaber lit up his face as it twirled a few times. He was circling, but he was circling closer. "Oh come on, Elly. Tell ya what. Let's put the lightsabers down and go get a drink, then we'll finish this."

I shook her head a little. "Nope. We'll finish this soon."

There was a crack and then I fell to the side, landing hard on the ground. "Ow! Shit!!"

Kent dropped his lightsaber and ran over to me. "Shit, Elly. Are you okay?"

I looked up at him with a grin and stabbed him under his armpit with my saber. "Sucka."

"Oh, dammit!" Kent laughed and fell to his knees and clutched his chest. "I will get my ...revenge.." He fell over on his side and played dead.

I jumped up and held my lightsaber over my head victoriously. "Yes!"

Mike and Paul shook their heads at Kent. "Dude, come on! I saw that coming from a mile away. You are so pussy whipped, and you aren't even getting any from her."

Paul chimed in, "Or are you?" He raised one eyebrow.

I ran at Mike and Paul and started whipping them on the legs with my lightsaber. "You ... guys ... are ... disgusting!"

Paul curled up and screamed like a little girl, "Stop!"

Mike started to run away and I was hot on his tail. "Come back here, you woman!" Mike was laughing too hard to outrun me and soon I was able to poke him in the ass with the end of my lightsaber. "I'll get you! You better call for someone to help you otherwise your ass is mine!"

Mike ran to a tree and then hid behind it. "Kent! Come get your girl off my ass. It's an exit only!"

Kent rolled over onto his back and pushed himself up from the ground, rubbing the dirt off of his pants. He walked over closer to us but made no moves to stop me.

"I dunno, dude. She might have the right to." Kent snickered.

"Damn straight I do, I'm the winner! Too bad you didn't win the special prize, Mike, or you could've had my ass," I teased.

Mike groaned and pounded his forehead against the tree. "Not fair."

"So what is your special prize, Elly?" Kent asked as he moved closer and put his arm around me to draw my attention away from Mike behind the tree.

"I get to pick the next activity, and who gets to tag along," I smiled sweetly, turning away from Mike and the tree shield.

Kent kept his arm on my shoulder and looked down at me. "So what is it going to be, sweetheart? Wait. Make that choice after we have some more booze!" Kent grabbed my hand and pulled me over to the limo to get some more liquor.

My eyes widened as I followed him. What the hell had happened to Kent? Suddenly he wanted to get hammered?

Mike came out from the tree and Paul climbed into the limo. He grabbed out the rest of the mini bar contents and held them out to everyone else getting in.

Kent took a bottle as he climbed into the limo and when I climbed in he took me by the hand and pulled me over to the seat beside him. He held his little bottle up to mine and slurred slightly. "Congo-rats" He downed the shot easily.

I grinned and then put mine in my lap. I was drunk enough I

wasn't going to have anymore until I knew I wouldn't black out but I surely wasn't going to stop the rest of them from having a good time. I held mine out to Kent. "Here, you missed one."

Kent shrugged his shoulders, a large grin on his lips, and drank it quickly. He coughed. "So,Elly.. what is the next thing going to be?"

"Video game competition at your mom's house. The junk food is waiting but the Dew has been replaced with jello shots." I smiled and looked around at the boys. "Everyone game?"

"Oh my gawd. More alcohol?" Kent chuckled. "Are you going to hold my hair later, Elly, when I throw up?"

I laughed at the thought. "Sure, I will." I looked at the other two who looked ready to sleep. "Are you two out?"

Kent looked at the other two. "Pussy number one!" He pointed at Mike. "And pussy number two." He pointed at Paul.

I bust out laughing.

Mike slapped his face and then Paul's. "Hell no, we ain't no pussies! Game on!"

Kent put his head back against the seat with a smug grin. "That's what I'm talking about!" Kent put his arm around me, squeezing softly. "Bestest party ever, Elly."

I pat his knee a couple of times. "That was the point." I grinned.

We arrived at Kent's house and piled out. I had asked Kent's mom to go over to my mom's house for the evening so we had the house to ourselves. The living room had been set up with bowls of chips, pretzels and Twizzlers in the middle. Four Gamecube controllers were evenly spaced out and there were four shot glasses next to them.

"Okay!" I went to the fridge and pulled out a six pack, bringing it back to the table. "Rules are: If you land on a blue space, you take a drink, land on a red space everyone else takes a drink. If you land on a special space you take two drinks. If you land on a Bowzer space everyone else takes two drinks. In the mini games the winner takes a drink and if it's a draw everyone takes a drink. And you do a jello shot whenever there is a star. Got it?!" I uncapped four beers and then sat down on the single chair, leaving Kent wedged between Mike and Paul on the couch.

"What the hell are we playin'?"

"Mario Party... OH!" I turned on the GameCube and then grabbed my controller, sitting back. "And for the last three rounds all the drinks are doubled."

"You're going to be holding my hair later, Elly." Kent laughed as he picked up his controller.

My mind went to the gutter for some reason and my face flushed. I cleared my throat and stared at the large TV screen.

"Lets get this party started! Woo!" I hadn't seen Kent like this in a very long time and it made my heart happy.

Halfway through the game, three beers, and three shots later per person, Mike and Paul were passed out. Mike had claimed he had to use the bathroom and ended up laying down on the kitchen floor. Paul laughed and then fell to the side on the love seat. He didn't have enough energy to get back up. And then there were two...I landed on a blue space. "Dammit!" I picked up my beer and took a sip, a very modest sip, but he probably wasn't paying attention.

Kent chuckled as he took his turn and landed on special square.

"Oh shit," he said as he picked up his beer. He took two very large gulps which finished the beer off. "This is...wow." He leaned back against the couch now that he had plenty of room. He put his head back against the cushion and began to sing, "Fuck You, I'm Drunk," softly. When he finished he snickered.

I sat back and watched him, a small smile on my lips. "When was the last time you were this drunk?"

"Uh.. Never." He ran his hands through his hair and made a low grumbling noise. Kent turned his head towards me. "I love you, Elly."

I held up my wrist to show him my tattoo. "I know."

"Are you gonna play or what, wench?" Kent stuck his tongue out at me and chuckled.

I gasped and stood up. I sat next to him after hitting the top of his head with a pillow. "Did you just call me a wench?"

"Yeah!" Kent laughed and turned his head to me. "You need to catch up."

I raised my eyebrows, "Catch up to what?" I picked up a controller and looked at the TV. A mini game popped up and it was Kent vs me again.

He sat up with his controller and tried hard. I beat him. "You drink more than I do. You have to at least be as fucked up as I am."

I grumbled as I took a tiny drink, "But I want to remember you like this."

Kent smirked as he looked at the screen. Three rounds left to go.

"Crap,everything is double." Kent played through on his turn and landed on a Bowser square. "Hah! Suck it! Double the double drink!"

I laughed and tipped back my beer four times, really only taking one gulp. "Alright, punk." I took my turn and landed on a star. "Ugh." I picked up two jello shots and sucked them down.

Kent went with two rounds left. He got us started on another mini game. I won this one too. Kent was snickering.

I sighed and finished off my beer and then bent down to get another. "Enjoying yourself?" I popped the top and set it down loudly on the table. My turn was a Bowzer and I grinned smugly.

"Having a blast," his mouth twisted into a drunken grin as he picked up the beer. He took four different large drinks and shook his head. "Belly can't take much more, too much in it. Wait! I'll be back!" He stood up from the couch and swayed a little bit as he made his way towards the downstairs bathroom.

I laid down, one arm over my eyes, the other on my stomach, "Oh god, Elly, what have you done?" I said to myself.

Chapter 29

Kent came back a few minutes later on his hands and knees and crawled with a snicker towards me, whispering, "Elly.. shh.." a little chuckle came out of him. "Lets go troll people in a chat!"

I pulled my arm away when I heard my name and laughed at him, still laying down, "Trolling? How old are we? Fifteen?" I rolled onto my side. "How about we go watch big boob porn instead?"

There was a shrug of his shoulders. "Okay," he said and started crawling towards the stairs that led up to his old room. Kent got to the stairs and used the hand rail to pull himself up. I followed behind him, giggling at his physical impairment.

Kent made it up the stairs and when we had to go past his mom's room, even though she wasn't there, he still put his finger up to his lips. "Shh..." He smiled and opened his door and went in. After I came in he shut the door. "Go start the computer up. I'm going to set the mood!" He chuckled to himself as I shook my head. Kent had turned the little lamp on when he'd come in, but now he went over and started lighting candles, very carefully around his room.

I headed for the computer. I turned it on and then turned around to watch him. I found myself biting my lower lip, hoping he wasn't going to burn down the house by accident.

Once the candles were lit, he swayed a little as he went and turned the lamp off. He moved over to the edge of his bed and took a seat. "You're in charge of the porn!"

"Ok...not sure you really want to do that but..." I turned around and moved my chair over so he could see the screen too from his position on the bed. I opened the browser history to see what was there, just like old times. I had to go way back in the browser history to find anything. What I found was not big boob porn but girls with average assets. Pretty girls that looked more normal than fake.

"What the hell, Kent? Where are the big boobs?"

"People grow out of stuff, Elly." He laughed.

I laughed. "You're gonna grow out of your pants in a few minutes."

"Whatever!" He shook his head and scratched his hand through his hair.

I clicked and typed and clicked again and finally there was a little movie on the screen. It was a cheerleader and a football player having sex. And just like every porn it started with the girl bobbing on the guy's dick.

Kent sat there on the edge of the bed and watched the screen of the monitor. His cheeks weren't blushing.

I glanced between him and the screen and closed the movie when I didn't see his blush. "Hmm...not working."

Kent raised his eyebrow at me and looked a little curious. "What's not working?"

I looked over my shoulder as I started another movie, one girl and four guys. I jumped ahead to the sex part. It was hardcore and the girl was loud. "Embarrassing you. Your cheeks aren't turning pink."

He smiled at me as his eyes shifted to the screen behind me. There was a little action before I caught his tongue running along his lips.

"Like this?" I asked. Kent was beginning to chew at his lip as he looked at me and then back at the screen. I glanced at his pants, noting the outline of something that wasn't there before. "I guess so." I grinned and shifted in my seat as I looked at the computer screen. It was hot, I had to admit.

"It's hot in here," he said as he pulled the shirt over his head with a little trouble. He dropped it on the floor and looked back at the screen.

I glanced back and realized immediately that it was a mistake seeing his naked torso. I turned back to the screen and started twirling my hair slowly between my fingers. "Getting hot and bothered back there?"

Kent snickered. "Maybe a little. Why you hiding over there, Elly?"

I shook my head and glanced at him briefly to try to prove that I wasn't. "I'm not hiding."

"Mhmm. You did your part now come watch the movie."

I pointed at the computer screen. "I am. I would say I have a better view than you, it's bigger up here."

"Being a size queen now, Elly?" He smirked and laid back on the bed. His pants looked like a tent. I looked away quickly. What was I doing?

"No, I mean it is pretty interesting. These guys things are ...impressive. And I didn't know a guy could last so long."

"Pfft. There are ways to last longer. It's not all about getting off in ten minutes."

I turned in my seat and looked at him. "Oh yeah? What ways are those?" Kent never wanted to talk about sex and now was my chance to pick his brain.

"I'll tell you but you have to come over here first." He pat the spot on the bed next to his thigh.

I shrugged off all those niggling thoughts telling me I shouldn't and went over to Kent. I sat down beside him, and put my hands in my lap. "Okay, now tell me."

"Oh, I don't know if I can tell you, my back is aching, it's all I can think about."

I rolled my eyes. "Oh my god, does that usually work on Jen? Because it's not going to work on me." I stood up and put my hands on my hips, looking down at his smirking face.

"No. I don't need to come up with lame lines for her to fall into bed with me. But you..." He grabbed my wrist and gently pulled it towards him. He tried to get my hand on his chest but I pulled away before it could.

"Yes, I'm not easy. Welcome to the world of Elly. If a guy wants to get into my pants he has to work for it..." I looked up at the ceiling briefly, admitting that I had a history of being easy, but that was in the past, mostly. "Well, nowadays anyway."

I looked back down to him and then tried to take a step back. His arm wrapped around my behind and pulled me roughly to him. We fell back onto the bed together, my boobs pressed against his bare chest. His dark eyes glittered in the low lighting and I sucked in a deep breath.

"Kent, what are you-" my words were interrupted by Kent's kiss. His lips pressed firmly against mine, I felt his fingers digging into my back, holding me in place against him.

I shook my head, turning my head to the side to prevent more kissing, "I can't. You won't remember any of it in the morning."

Kent looked up at me with his eyes full of lust. "I'll remember." His hips pressed up so his erection ground against me again. "How could I forget this? How could I forget you giving this to me?"

My eyes fluttered closed, my cheeks flushed. I felt his hand move up into my hair and felt his fist tighten within it. That hand pulled my head down so our lips could meet again. I was like putty in his hands, the submissive between us. I let him kiss me, waiting for my mind to shut off and stop telling me how wrong this was. The kiss was broken by him as he nipped at my bottom lip.

"Just give in already, Elly. Let your body do what it wants." His other hand slid down and moved under my shirt, his hot fingers touching the soft skin of my side.

I swallowed hard, my eyes still closed. Could I do this again? Could I throw my heart into the fire, letting it possibly get burned up? I was frozen there, my hands on his chest. "Kent..."

He shifted on the bed with me so that he was on top of me. The hand in my hair moved to the back of my neck and pulled my head forward for a more forceful kiss. His hand on my side skimmed under my shirt until it almost touched my sports bra.

I shivered underneath him, a soft moan escaping me as his hand and lips claimed me, burning my skin, sending pulses of fire between my thighs. My legs closed around his waist unconsciously and I squeezed him, lifting my hips wanting release already.

The kiss held and his hand moved up to take hold of one of my breasts. Kent pressed his hips against me to let me feel his erection again.

My hips moved up and then down, my center rubbing against his erection. I moaned against his lips, my hands moving to the back of his head, gripping his neck tight as I kissed him back. The want getting hotter and harder to resist. He leaned back after breaking the kiss, moving his hand between our bodies, rubbing my sweet spot.

My eyes were still closed, my back arched as my feet fell to the bed, releasing my hold on him. My hips thrust up, trying to force the friction to my liking. "Oh god, Kent!"

He let me control the friction for a moment before both of his hands met at the band of my spandex pants. They were yanked down past my hips and his hand thrust back between my thighs. I gasped as he pushed my thong to the side, his finger brushing between my curls.

My hands went to his hair, pulling at it as I rolled my hips. He lowered his head as his other hand lifted my shirt just a little so he could kiss my stomach. My thighs tried to close to capture his arm. Kent placed a soft kiss under my belly button. I felt his teeth catch the soft flesh of one of my thighs as he allowed one finger to slide inside of me.

"Don't you want me? Don't you want to feel me deep inside you?"

The breath from his words tickled the inside of my thigh. I gasped, gripping his hair tighter, my body so responsive beneath his.

"Yes...yes."

I started to buck my hips but resisted, pushing my hips back down when they were halfway up. I raised my head and looked down at him in the dimly lit flickering light, his dark eyes looked up into mine. I knew I'd never forget the image of him between my thighs.

The computer screen had gone black into power save mode, and the only light was from the flickering candles, but there was still enough of it. A smile moved along his lips as his head lowered and his tongue moved along with his finger. His tongue began to tease my clit while his finger moved in and out of me. The whole time his eyes kept looking into mine.

It was too much, too intense, my head dropped back onto his pillow, my hands still tense in his hair as he ate me out. My hips moved up and down in a slow rhythm. I felt his slick finger sliding in and out of my tightness, his tongue on me caused little white bursts behind my eyelids.

It felt so fucking good, the best thing I'd ever felt. I never, ever wanted it to end. My hips stuttered as I tried to break the rhythm, trying to make myself last longer. My loud moans filled the room.

His finger and tongue stopped moving. I could hear him speak and feel his hot breath below the belt. "Ask me. Ask me to get you off."

My body was glistening with a light sheen, the exertion from resisting my orgasm showing on my skin. I lifted my head and looked down at him. I kept my lips pressed together, a little frown on my face as I lifted my hips, trying to shut him up with my wet heat.

He slid down more on the bed and his arms moved around either hip. His hands came to rest on my thighs where his fingers pressed into my skin. His face buried against my crotch as his tongue pushed between my lips and wiggled inside of me.

I gasped loudly and tried to wiggle away from him, "Kent!..."

My hands had lost his hair and gripped the bedspread beside my hips tightly. His face pressed against me as his tongue moved around inside of me.

My body curled up, my strings as tight as they could be, my explosion on the brink of happening. "Wait, Kent, wait!..."

Kent paused for a moment, kissing the inside of my thigh. I panted softly, letting myself uncoil and cool down. I looked down at him.

"You taste so good, Elly. Why do you want me to stop?"

Him saying that was a huge turn on, I groaned, "Um..." I was stalling, "Uh..." I bit my lower lip.

"If you can't tell me I'm going to keep going." He said as his tongue ran over my lips just once. I shivered and lifted my hips, moaning loudly. "Um..."

Again his face buried in my crotch. His tongue was unrelenting as it wiggled inside of me and his fingers gripped my thighs. I let out a little scream as he devoured me, and finally I blew. My body spasmed and gushed as he forced my orgasm from me. My hips raised and then fell, trying to stop the sweet pain.

"Fuck!"

His fingers gripped my thighs harder to keep me from getting away. My screams turned into pants. My body was wound up so tight that I let out little whimpers every time his tongue stroked me.

"Oh!...Please!"

And then another orgasm ripped from me and I screamed out again, my body seizing up for a moment and then shaking with my release. My legs squeezed together tightly as I pushed his head away.

"No more...please...Mercy!..."

Kent finally let go of my thighs and moved up my body, his body dragging against mine. I felt his lips on mine as he hungrily kissed me. It was shocking and hot at the same time. I kissed him back passionately, tasting myself on his lips. My hands went to his back, my nails digging in slightly when he rubbed against me, sending a spasm through my body.

"Can you taste yourself?" he whispered against my lips as he leaned back. Kent's hands went for the button of his pants as his tongue moved along his lips.

I nodded, my hands on the back of his pants, pushing them down eagerly as soon as they were loose. "Yes."

"Can you taste how sweet you are?" His dick was rock hard and pushed against his boxers eager to be let out.

I nodded again, whispering, "Yes...that was...that was amazing."

"I want to show you more," he said in an almost whisper. His dark eyes didn't seem to be able to look away from mine.

His hand came down and opened his boxers so his cock could be free. He leaned forward, his hands went to either side of me to support his weight. His length was sliding and throbbing against me. The action brought a little moan out of him.

My hands moved to his forearms, gripping them tightly, my eyes on his.

"We should stop," I whispercd, my breath hitching in my throat when he accidentally slipped into me.

There was a pause for just a moment as his body shuddered with excitement. Those eyes of his were looking deep into mine as his hips pressed forward so he went farther in. My cheeks flushed, my fingers tightened on his arms but I held still, gasping as he went in further still.

"You're so tight, Elly." The words came out as a whisper through his lips. He slid all the way in until he couldn't go anymore. That was when he started to pull out of me slowly.

I closed my eyes against his image, trying to enjoy it without my thoughts clouding it.

"Kent, we should..." I whimpered when he slammed into me, knocking me back into the bed.

Kent moaned with pleasure. My hands moved to his hips and I tried to push them away, my mind was jumbling as his hot tongue penetrated my mouth, flicking at my tongue.

My hands on his hips gripped him as he sped up, my fingernails digging into the muscular flesh of his back. I moaned as he pushed deeper inside of me. I turned my head so I could moan his name.

"God, you feel so good, Elly," he said softly into my ear, nibbling it.

"How good?" I whispered, whimpering every time he thrust into me and filled me up.

"All I want to do...is lose myself with you." The words hitched in his throat and he moaned. He gave me a moment of hard fucking before he let it slow down again. He moaned my name.

I reached down and grabbed his ass, pulling him towards my body, "Harder again, please..."

His hips came down, meeting with mine, the sound of our skin slapping together echoed within the room. The feeling of his ass working so hard under my palms turned me on even more. He felt so good inside me. I wanted to explode for him but I just wasn't there yet.

"Yes!" I gasped out.

He lowered his head and bit at my breast still hidden behind my shirt.

My breaths came out as gasps and moans as he fucked the shit out of me.

"Oh god...Oh...god..."

As he pounded into me, my insides started to sizzle. My mind went to Kent's tongue on me and I felt the snap as I cracked, my body writhed beneath his. I let out a scream of pleasure, my fists closing tight.

"Oh...shit..." Kent whispered as his eyes closed.

I felt his body shiver as his thrusts became harder. I felt that jolt of him exploding inside of me. His body jerked and his arm moved to behind me, his fingers gripping my waist tightly.

I panted softly as I caught my breath. My hand moved through his hair slowly as his head rested against my shoulder as he tried to slow his breath.

When he pulled out I moved over and put a hand on my forehead. "What did we do?"

Kent fell onto his back. I rolled over again onto my side, facing him.

"Seriously, what did we do? What was that? What...what are we going to do with that?"

Kent turned his head towards me with a smile. "What do you mean?"

"I mean...are you still getting married in three days?"

Kent looked tired, but he had heard me. His head turned upward toward the ceiling. I took that as his answer. I rolled towards him and put my cheek to his chest. "It's ok...I...understand."

"Elly," His hand came to my back and started to rub it. "We'll talk about it in the morning. I just," Kent seemed uncertain.

I pressed a kiss to his chest and then put my cheek back where it was. "Let's get some rest." I wasn't ready to face the rejection just yet. He reached down and pulled the sheet up so we were covered. The last few candles flickered and went out and I finally closed my eyes letting sleep take me.

Chapter 30

I moaned softly as I woke up. The place between my thighs was sore from the encounter I'd had with Kent. I thought briefly that maybe it was dream. I turned over, smiling, expecting to touch his chest. But all I felt was a cold sheet. I opened my eyes and looked around. The door was closed and Kent wasn't in the room.

I wondered if his mom had come back. I wrapped the sheet around myself and ventured out into the hallway. The house was quiet. I crept downstairs and looked around carefully, I didn't want to be caught by Kent's mom wearing just a sheet. I saw no signs of Mike or Paul. I glanced at the clock and groaned, it was almost ten. I ran back upstairs, grabbed my clothes and got in the shower. As I was dressing I heard the door close downstairs. I crept into the hallway carefully, hiding upstairs to eavesdrop.

I heard Kent's mom set her purse and keys on the kitchen counter, where there was space, it was still littered with empty beer bottles and half eaten bags of junk food.

I heard Kent say, "Mom, what is it?"

She was silent for awhile, "What are you doing, son?"

"I'm standing in the kitchen and feeling rather full from brunch. What else would I be doing?" He was playing dumb, that was good, maybe. Probably not, his mom wasn't going to drop it.

"No, darling boy. I meant with Elly." My breath caught in my throat. "What are you doing? Are you going to be a no-show at the wedding? Because it would be better, as hard as it might be, to end it now instead."

"What are you talking about, mom? You came in on me and Elly sleeping in bed together lots of times."

I closed my eyes tightly, fighting back the tears as my heart slammed in my chest.

"So you aren't sleeping with her?" She sounded surprised, partially relieved.

"Mom, nothing happened."

I crept back to the bathroom.

She let out a deep sigh. "Thank god. I thought I was going to have to call everyone and tell them they shouldn't fly in for the wedding."

I closed the bathroom door loudly and went down the hallway, wiping at my eyes, refusing to cry. I knew this was probably going to happen. I had hoped it wouldn't but deep down I knew it would.

I came downstairs and looked at Kent's mom. "Thanks for letting us use your place last night, Mrs. Lytle. I was hoping to have it cleaned up before you guys got back."

Kent's mom turned and smiled at me, pretending I hadn't just been the topic of conversation. "That's okay, sweetheart. When I left this morning your mom told me that you two had plans for lunch? You should get going so you're not late."

I nodded, slipped my shoes on, bag in hand. I headed for the front door, calling out to Kent over my shoulder since he couldn't be bothered to acknowledge me. "See you at the wedding, Mr. Groom."

"Thanks, Elly." He yelled back at me.

He was obviously feeling guilty for sleeping with me during his drunken stupor, and I was feeling guilty for falling for it. For being so stupid. For expecting more from him.

* * *

The wedding day had arrived. The weather was unusually warm for New Year's Eve and all the seats inside the grand ballroom were filled. When it was almost time the wedding planner queued Kent to take his place at the front. From up there he could see everyone's face. Everyone was there. And I was seated in the middle on his side, Stacy as my plus one sitting beside me. When his eyes locked on me I offered him a little smile and a thumb's up. He offered me a little smile and then turned his gaze on his mom.

When the pipe organ started it caused Kent to jump a little. The videographer, luckily, was pointed at the bridesmaids and groomsmen as they came down the aisle.

Once they were in their places, the flower girl, a young cousin of Jen's, came down. She threw flowers gracefully for the first few rows as the wedding planner had instructed her to do and then sat down next to her mother in the front row.

The wedding march started and Jen appeared at the back of the long aisle. She was beautiful, all eyes were on her, even mine. Stacy leaned over and whispered into my ear but I wasn't listening to what she'd said, I was too distracted. Jen walked gracefully down the aisle in her Vera Wang dress which was just the right amount of innocence and sex appeal.

One by one the rows of people turned as Jen walked past. She was smiling at her guests until finally she reached the alter. She looked at Kent and took his nervous hands in hers, which were shaking too. She flashed him a smile and let out a little exhale to try to calm her nerves.

Kent let the smile stay as best he could but his stomach was flopping around on his insides, and it was obvious, to me anyway.

I didn't stay for the whole ceremony but I caught most of it. I departed just before "I do."

* * *

There was a slight puffing on the mic as I tapped it softly. I looked out at the crowd and my eyes found Mike who was staring at me dressed in a formal gold evening gown. I didn't even really look like myself because of the makeup and the hair. I had a guitar strapped on me and my band was behind me, the only familiar thing in this uncomfortable wedding hall.

"Good evening everyone. We're here to celebrate the marriage of Mr. and Mrs. Jen and Kent Lytle. We're going to start things off right with their wedding song. Kent, Jen...please come on up to the dance floor." I looked at them and motioned to the dance floor and then turned my back to the floor for a moment.

The band wasn't playing for this one, just me. I softly strummed my guitar as I waited for them to get into position. When Jen's arms went to Kent's shoulders I started crooning "At Last."

I couldn't look at the happy couple, arms around each other, it was going to throw me off my gig. The gig I didn't even really want in the first place. Jen approached me yesterday and asked if I wouldn't mind playing at the reception because her other band cancelled on her. I focused on the lyrics as I ended the song. I set my guitar down.

"And now for the father-daughter dance." Jen's dad came up and took Jen away from Kent and started to dance when I started singing "When The Stars Go Blue." The rest of the band joined in for this one. I glanced around the room, catching sight of Kent by the bar, Paul's friendly hand patting him in congratulations.

The song ended and I waited for the applause before speaking, "And the last dance for the wedding party only. The mother-son dance. I wasn't given a song for this dance so I picked it myself. I hope you like it, Kent and Mrs. Lytle. Please come on out to the dance floor." My eyes stayed mostly on Kent's mom, darting to Kent for a brief second every minute or so.

The beautiful guitar started, the drum cymbals crashed softly and then I started to sing "The First Time Ever I Saw Your Face." I watched Kent and his mother circling slowly around the dance floor , closing my eyes when I got to the second verse. I didn't want Jen to think I was singing it to him, which I totally was.

The applause filled the room as the song ended. After it died down I spoke again, "Now the bride and groom would like to invite everyone else to join them on the dance floor." We started our pop music set and I was smiling, enjoying watching everyone dance. I was so entranced that I didn't even notice when Kent and Jen disappeared.

A half an hour and a bottle of water later I took a break from the stage and made my way to the bathroom. I knocked on the door, there was no answer so I knocked on the door again and jiggled the handle impatiently. I really had to pee!

"Be out in.. a minute. The p-p-punch isn't sitting well..."

I sighed softly and leaned against the wall, crossing my ankles to keep the fluids in.

I heard a grunt in the bathroom and turned my eyes suspiciously to the door. What the hell?

The door opened after another minute and Jen came out, a devilish smile on her made up lips. "Hey, Elly. Sorry about that."

I tried to hide my frown as I opened the door and I gasped as my eyes met with Kent's, his hands on his pants.

"Oh, sorry!" I retreated and stood outside the door, waiting for him to vacate.

As I stood there I couldn't help but replay our night together. He'd had his chance, and he let it slip through his fingers. It had hurt. It still hurt, my heart was still raw. Despite how much I'd changed it wasn't enough to keep him. He must have really loved Jen. Maybe I wasn't slutty enough for him. I certainly wouldn't get on my knees in my wedding dress and give him a blow job at our wedding reception. I couldn't face him and let him see the hurt on my face. I quickly walked away, there had to be another bathroom somewhere.

The rest of the wedding went rather quickly. I stood at the back of the crowd and watched Jen kiss Kent. And Kent kiss Jen. They kissed an awful lot. They looked as happy as a couple should on their wedding day. I wrapped my arms around myself and forced myself watch the scene before me. I had to tape it to the top of the box that held the romantic Kent memories. He'd had her, he'd had me, and he chose her. That chapter was closed. I needed to move on.

I watched the limo drive away with them in it. And with it went my heart.

Keep Reading For A Sneak Peek at Part Two: Old Friends

TEN YEARS LATER...

Chapter 1

I wasn't necessarily looking forward to tonight - the food was going to be wonderful but Jen's birthday dinners were always so joyless. She pretended to like the gifts we gave her but she was not very good at it. She'd long since dropped her public face around me. She reserved that for newcomers, acquaintances - tonight she'd be in the presence of unknown company so I was hopeful that we could all be civil and enjoy ourselves a little bit.

Despite everything we'd been through since high school I'd somehow managed to be civil towards her. We were far from BFFs but we did exchange an occasional email every now and again, mostly about Kent..

Several years after college I met a terrific guy and we dated for a couple of years. He moved away for work and I stayed behind without him. The relationship with him proved to me that I could love someone despite the trampling my heart had taken in my youth. A year later I met Dave at one of my wedding gigs. He flirted with me shamelessly and because he was so funny, intelligent and charming, I gave in. It probably hadn't hurt that he was extremely hot.

Tonight marked two months since Dave and I started dating and this was the first time I decided to let him meet any of my friends. If he could survive Jen and Kent, then he could survive anyone.

I inhaled deeply and expelled my breath slowly, letting the tension and anxiety leave me before I stepped out of the cab to greet my uber-handsome date, Dave. I tugged on the bottom of my hot pink hem, pulling it closer to my knees. I flashed Dave a reassuring smile as I took the arm he held out to me. He looked yummy in his sleek dark blue Calvin Klein suit. His crisp white shirt was flashing beneath and matched his perfect, straight, white teeth.

He bent down slightly to whisper against my ear, "You look stunning. Do your panties match your shoes?"

I looked down at my black high heels, scoffed and then laughed softly. I squeezed his bicep and gave him a sideways glance, trying to remain coy. "If you're a good boy, maybe you'll find out. So tell me again, who are we meeting for dinner?"

He rubbed his nose into my pulled back hair, kissed the top of my head and then groaned. We'd practiced their names at least a dozen times already. "Jen and Kent, your two old high school friends."

I grinned at him and grabbed his tie, pulling him down for a quick kiss.

"That's right. And what topics are we avoiding tonight?" I asked.

His hazel eyes flashed gold as he stared down into mine. He spoke low, his voice sending little flickers through my body, "Kids, and anything involving you."

I nodded and rewarded him with another kiss, this one a little longer, our lips grazing softly, drawing out into longer kisses. It was interrupted by a man clearing his throat loudly.

I stepped to the side and pulled back when I realized Kent and Jen were standing there staring at us.

Kent was dressed in a suit, he looked handsome but extremely uncomfortable, he kept pulling at his collar. He had a large purple present under his left arm, the silver bow sparkled in the subdued lights of the street.

I pasted on my happy face and hugged Jen. "Happy Birthday, Birthday Girl!" I gave her an extra squeeze and then stepped back.

She smiled softly, it almost reached her eyes, and looked between me and my date. "Thank you. You look great, Elly. Better than I do tonight, don't you think, Ken?"

She looked at her husband and nudged him to get his papa-bear glare off from Dave.

He didn't even glance at me, avoided looking at me entirely. Had it been a decade ago I would've been offended, but as it was I was used to his avoidance in the presence of others. It was just the way he was since the night we don't ever bring up.

"No, of course not, Jen. Don't be silly. You look terrific," he said with a tiny smile.

She did. She looked sophisticated in her split neck knee-length blue dress. I always admired how she always seemed to look so put together. Even if she showed up at Kent's work after hitting the gym in a t-shirt she would end up looking like an Adidas advertisement. Kent leaned in to press a kiss to her cheek but she pulled back.

"Make-up." She smiled sweetly to play off the blatant rejection of his affections and then nodded towards the door of the fancy Italian restaurant. "Shall we? Our reservation won't keep for much longer."

We walked, single file, into Amici. I felt my shoulders tighten as Dave's warm hand moved to my lower back. I wasn't too keen on his constant need to touch a part of my body any time we were in public, which was always because there was something that was niggling me about him. I just couldn't put my finger on what it was.

After we were seated and the waiter departed with our drink orders, Jen smiled sweetly to us.

"So, how are you guys doing?" Kent asked. I watched as Kent's eyes shifted from me to Dave and then to the silverware on the table. The present was sitting on the table beside Jen, who payed no attention to it.

I spoke up after smiling to Dave, dividing my attention as evenly as I could between my three dinner companions.

"We're good. Dave moved into a those new apartments across from the Town Centre last week. He's on the 15th floor and the view is absolutely amazing..." I paused and took a sip of water, my throat feeling as parched as the desert as I tried to bring some life and cheer to the table.

I felt Dave's eyes on me, and when I glanced at him they seemed to simmer as he watched my lips puckering on the frosty glass.

Jen beamed at us from across the table. "Sounds amazing. We're still over on Bridge Street but you already knew that. Nothing new. I spend all day at home while Ken runs his businesses. It's the life of a rich man's wife, it seems." Jen always dropped the T off of Kent's name. It forever annoyed me, but I always kept it to myself.

Dave laughed softly, "So, do you sit around and watch TV and eat bon-bons all day? That's what stay-at-home wives do, isn't it?"

I laughed softly at the question and shook my head. I was curious what Jen's response was going to be and snuck a glance at Kent, catching him smirking briefly.

Kent spoke up first, "Ordering movies on pay-per-view, going shopping, ordering things on the internet...I think that about covers it, wouldn't you say?" His arm was on the back of her chair as he looked at her.

She frowned a little as she reached over and puckered his cheeks between her fingers. "You forgot cooking, my dear. I make a mean frozen pizza."

Jen winked at Dave and Kent shook his head, his gaze firmly on Jen.

"Oh yes, Mr. P's for the win," he muttered.

Dave gave Kent a once over and shrugged. "Doesn't look like she starves you. How is it having a wife as hot as yours waiting at home for you every night?"

He put his arm around me and tugged me gently against his side. I winced briefly but smiled to cover the discomfort of leaning over the space between our chairs.

"Some day soon I hope I'll have a wife of my own at home." Dave stared down at me and I glanced up to meet his eyes.

He had that look there. A look of longing, of promises. I was starting to feel a bit panicky. I pressed a kiss to his lips and then pulled back.

"It's wonderful. I look forward to it every day when I close up the shop. It's something everyone should wish for. Elly would make a good wife." Kent leaned over to try to give Jen a kiss on the cheek but stopped. "Right, make-up. Excuse me while I go to the restroom." Kent slid his chair out and stood from the table just as the waiter dropped off our drinks.

I watched Kent briefly as he stood up from the table before turning my attention back to Jen.

"What are you and Kent doing this weekend?"

"Well, he has his third shop opening next Saturday so he'll probably be there all weekend to get things set and do the training. So I guess that means I'm free!" She grinned at both of us, looking expectantly.

I looked between Jen and Dave and put my hand on Dave's knee and gave it a gentle squeeze. "I'm busy Saturday too. Booked for two weddings."

Dave sighed, "Right, I forgot. I'll miss you." He leaned down and pressed a kiss to my cheek.

I felt my cheeks color and smiled at Jen. "You're not going to the store opening?"

She shook her head. "What's there for me? Computer nerds ogling my goods and women hitting on Ken who don't deserve his attention? No, I'll keep my jealousy to myself, thanks." Jen laughed softly as my fists clenched together tightly under the table as she left the 'T' off his name.

Kent returned to the table and took his seat once again. "Sorry. What did I miss?" He asked as Jen turned her face to look at him.

"Oh, I told them your new shop was opening. Said you'd be busy."

I noticed Kent's ears were turning a little red and shifted in my seat. His ears only did that when it was cold out or when he was getting angry. It wasn't very cold in the restaurant.

"I see. So not much of anything, then," Kent said.

I glanced at Dave who was looking just as uncomfortable as I was with the marital tension on the opposite side of the table.

I cleared my throat and pointed to the speakers overhead, "Oh, I love this song. I wish I spoke Italian. You speak some, don't you, Dave?"

Dave received my signal loud and clear and nodded, "A little. Jen, Kent, do you speak any languages?"

The married couple glared at each other for a moment but then Dave's question sunk in and the tension was gone. Jen was the first to answer, she kept her gaze pointed at Dave. "No, I don't speak anything other than English, and I'm bad at that most days. Kent speaks a few, but I don't hear him speaking them much around the house anymore."

Kent cleared his throat as the coloring in his ears was starting to fade. "I speak C++ and Basic." He didn't wait for the pause to his computer nerd joke, "I also speak French and a bit of Latin." Kent shrugged his shoulders nonchalantly, as if he weren't as amazing as I still knew him to be. As a person, not a man.

"Kent is too smart for his britches. Always has been." I grinned, trying to lighten the mood.

Dave laughed. "Yeah? I went into business because that computer stuff was too daunting."

"For you and me, both." I nudged Dave with my elbow playfully.

"Kent ended up with his Master's in that computer stuff and a minor in Language Arts. I told him he should have been a teacher...I think he would have liked that better."

Kent turned to Jen and smiled coldly. They had this argument before too. Kent saw the dollar signs in Jen's eyes and made every effort to give them to her. Jen ate it up and kept asking for more. "Maybe I should have. I don't know. Some days are better than others, right?" He looked at us for support.

I smiled. "I'm not sure anyone loves their job every minute of it." Dave's fingers captured my right ear and gently starting moving his fingers over it.

"Except you, right, Els?" Dave asked.

I looked at Dave after putting my shoulder to my ear to stop him from stroking it. "Even I have bad days at work."

Kent sipped his tea and then spoke up, "How is the singing treating you, Elly? We've...well, I've been so busy with the new store that we haven't had much of a chance to talk."

That much was true. Their wedding spurred a huge jump in my wedding singing career. I had thought, at the time, that it would be a great way to earn some extra money. Almost a decade later and I was still doing large events along with open mic nights when I wasn't waiting tables, which was my day job. Between the two I had enough to pay the bills and very little time for a social life.

"It's going well. I wish more people would have weddings during the week, but," I shrugged, chuckling softly. "I'll take what I can get. Excuse me, I have to use the ladies room."

Chapter 2

Once alone, I stared at myself in the mirror and pulled out my phone. I groaned as I noted that we'd only been seated for twenty minutes. It felt more like eighty. I freshened up my face, checked my email, and shot Stacy a text.

ME: OMG. THESE BIRTHDAY DINNERS ARE THE WORST!

STACY: ARE U TEXTING AT THE TABLE? RUDE!

ME: I'M IN THE LADIES. HAHA. HAD TO TAKE A BREATHER. JEN IS ALREADY ON HER SECOND COCKTAIL.

STACY: IT'S HER BIRTHDAY. GIVE HER A BREAK.

ME: *ROLLS EYES* WHATEVS. DO I HAVE 2 GO BACK?

STACY: YES! CALL ME LATER! :-*

When I came back there was an odd tension at the table. I sat down and was about to ask what I'd missed when the food arrived. We all ate dinner and made small talk.

When it was time for dessert the waiter came to our table with a gang of wait staff behind him, the chocolate cake slice glittered on the plate, leading the way. They all sang "Happy Birthday" and clapped when it ended. Jen closed her eyes and blew out her candle.

"What did you wish for, Jen?" Kent grinned as he sat back, rubbing his stomach as if he were full, which seemed odd because he'd barely eaten anything. Jen sucked the chocolate from the candle and I couldn't help but wonder if she was trying to seduce Kent or Dave. Neither would surprise me and I resisted the strong urge to roll my eyes.

"You know Jen can't tell you or her wish won't come true. I think it's present time!" I nodded to the large purple present which I'd wanted to open since I'd seen it.

Jen apparently didn't need further prodding. She grabbed the present and ripped the paper open despite Kent's attempt at speaking up to say something about the gift. He smiled at her excitement of opening the present, purple paper flew everywhere.

Peeking from the box was a slight sparkle. She pulled the dress out and held it up to her chest. The low-cut v-neck was embellished with hundreds of tiny diamonds. Kent was smiling as he watched her.

"Happy Birthday, Jen! It's from Elly and I."

I was about to speak up but held my tongue. I had nothing to do with that gift to Jen and the one in my purse seemed severely inadequate after Kent's extravagant purchase.

Dave whistled. "That's quite a dress."

She examined it and nodded slowly, "Yes...it's uh...something!" I could clearly see the false smile as she looked at me, "What do you think, Elly? Does it look good?"

I nodded with an approving smile, "Yes, it's beautiful." I glanced at Kent whose lips fell slightly at Jen's less than enthusiastic reply.

Jen looked between us, "Thanks, Elly and Kent. Maybe I'll wear it around town tomorrow!" She laughed and then put the dress back into the box, daintily tapping the top once it was secured.

Kent nodded at his wife, "You're welcome. Well. If you guys want to hang out a little more, you can. I need to get home since I have an early start to the day tomorrow. It was really nice of you guys to come out on such short notice." Kent was pretty much just talking to me.

I smiled softly and then turned my glance to Jen. "I wouldn't have missed it for the world." I looked at Dave who nodded at me that he wanted to leave and we stood. "Happy Birthday again. I hope you have a good night," I said as I walked around the table and hugged Jen one last time to seal the friendly relationship for another year.

Dave held his hand out to Kent for a shake, "Nice to meet you, Kent."

"Nice to meet you too, Dave." Kent returned the handshake.

Jen squeezed me tightly for a moment and kissed me on the cheek. She whispered softly into my ear so that only I could hear. "Have fun tonight."

After those words she picked up the box and moved to stand by Kent. Kent moved around and put his arms around me, surrounding me with his warmth.

"Good to see you as always. Maybe we can do lunch later in the week. That is, if you bring it by work." His words weren't too loud because Jen still turned green if Kent and I spent time alone without her. Although she no longer had anything to fear from me.

The whole year after their marriage I kept my distance, trying to get myself together after the heartache. It took me a long time to be able to be in the same room with him without wanting to burst into tears.

Kent had never pushed for a reason why, but I had made myself scarce with work which was good enough for him as a newlywed man and a brand new entrepreneur.

As their second anniversary rolled around I had finally come to terms with the fact that Kent was a friend. Just a friend. And that's all he would ever be. By their fifth anniversary I finally made him into a eunuch in my mind, and it was so much easier to be around him. After I started waiting tables downtown near Kent's new computer store I brought him lunch. It gave us time to rekindle our friendship in the safe environment of his business.

I grinned and pulled away after a brief two seconds of contact. "If you're lucky. Make me proud, Kent. Be extra nice to your wife."

I winked at Kent and then stepped back beside Dave and waved goodbye. With our goodbyes said we parted ways at the door. Kent walked with Jen towards the SUV and opened the door for her. He gave one last wave to me and then disappeared from view.

I turned my attention back to Dave. "I think I'm going to have to ask for a raincheck for dessert tonight." I pressed a kiss to his lips and then stepped back, taking in his playful pout.

"Alright, that's two desserts that you owe me. I'm very good at keeping records," he said.

I smiled and let my hands drop from his as I took slow, careful steps backwards so my black heels wouldn't catch on anything. "So am I." I winked at him and then slowly walked away, leaving him without a goodbye. Every man loved a little hard-to-get.

Chapter 3

I cursed myself for the third time as the cold wind bit at my exposed goose-fleshed arms. I ate a little too much at dinner and decided to walk back to my apartment instead of taking a cab. I had learned mid-way through college that the key to having a hot body was through moderation and keeping the calorie count down. And the only two ways to reduce the calories were to starve or exercise. I found that I preferred the exercise but as the wind hit me again I was rethinking my decision. Surely skipping breakfast tomorrow would be less painful than this.

I was halfway home when I spotted Kent's SUV parked on the curb in front of Bella, the upscale dress shop that Kent had probably purchased that extravagant dress from. I almost passed by Jen without noticing that she was sitting outside on the black wrought iron bench because I was busily looking for them inside the store.

I heard Jen whisper, "Elly?" I whipped my head around and then came back to sit beside Jen, whose mascara was running, her eyes slightly puffy from crying.

"Jen, hey, why are you crying? What happened?"

I looked over her depleted form, she looked every bit like a human being at that moment and much less like the rich untouchable socialite that she always projected. My hand rubbed over her back to comfort her and I wondered what the hell had happened in the past forty-five minutes to make her look so gutted. And I also wondered where the hell Kent was.

She had a tissue to her nose and mouth and made a little quivering sob, "Ken and I, we're just so miserable. I don't make him happy anymore and I don't know what I can do. He's so distant, he works all the time. I was actually surprised that he even bothered to show up for my birthday dinner this year. We used to have so much fun together. He used to be funny, carefree..."

I just listened, letting her get it all out. There was no use trying to defend Kent, it would appear that I was on his side and honestly, I didn't want to be on anyone's side. This was their marriage, not mine. My aim had always been to be a listening ear.

"And that dress was just ridiculous. Where would I even wear something like that? I've been hinting for months that what I wanted was a vacation, a second honeymoon. And instead he blows our money on a gaudy diamond encrusted dress. He said he wanted me to have something that would match my beauty and worth to him but that was just his cover up. He doesn't want to go away with me. He doesn't want to be alone with me." She started to sob again and I held back a sigh.

This was not the first time I'd heard this complaint from Jen. She didn't seem to understand that Kent was working his ass off for her. She was used to living a certain way and he was trying his damnedest to live up to her expectations. Jen was a smart woman, always had been, and I truly felt she needed something else in her life to distract her so she didn't hold her magnifying glass over Kent and her marriage 24/7.

She'd clung to Kent and made her life revolve around acquiring and keeping him. She used to have school to fill in the times when she wasn't with him. But after college and marriage she just stayed home claiming she wanted to make a nice house for Kent and that she didn't want to quit her career midyear when she finally got pregnant again. The pregnancy never happened and nine years later here we were. Both of them seemed miserable. But as Switzerland I kept my opinions to myself.

I continued to rub her back and looked over my shoulder into the store once more. "Where did he go? Is he inside?"

She let a humorless laugh escape her throat. "No, he ran off, like a coward. Even after bulking up and getting rid of the geeky glasses he still hasn't lost that trait. He still runs away from confrontation."

"He probably just needed some time to cool off. He'll come back for you."

"Maybe he will, maybe he won't. I won't be here to find out. I'm going to spend the rest of my birthday doing something fun."

She straightened up and pushed her long blonde hair over her slim shoulder. I couldn't help but smile. She was an expert at bouncing back.

"That a girl!" I put my hands flat on the bench on either side of me and sat up straight too. She was still about half a foot taller than I was. She turned my way as she dabbed away the runny mascara.

"Elly, why didn't you fight for Kenny?"

I felt my cheeks color. I really didn't want to discuss what I considered to be the most embarrassing time of my life.

I shrugged my shoulders and pasted on a smile, "He didn't want me, Jen. He wanted you. He picked you, over and over again."

I made sure I emphasized that for both our sakes. It was easy to romanticize the past, and think back and remember things that weren't truthful.

"I always thought he wanted you. Sometimes I still wonder if he does." She stuffed the used tissue into her large designer purse and stood up.

I stood up too, "You're just hurt. You'll see things clearly tomorrow. Kent loves you. He adores you. How could he not?" I smiled again and reached out, squeezing her elbow affectionately.

She smiled back and sighed softly, looking at the ground in shame. "I'm sorry, Elly. You're right. You're such a good friend."

She hugged me, tail between her legs so to speak. I smiled for her sake as she pulled back and straightened up, the rich bitch face back on.

"Now for my fun. Do you want to come with?"

"I'd love to but I have to be up early for work in the morning. Drink a Long Island for me." I grinned as I watched her walk around the SUV.

She opened the driver's side and paused, "Will do! Thanks for coming tonight, Elly. I hope to see more of you and Dave. You two look really great together."

She smiled a little, waved and then got in and closed the door. I watched as she pulled away from the curb and sighed heavily. I had one more stop to make and it was going to be too long to walk. When she was out of sight I hailed a cab.

Chapter 4

I paid the taxi driver and got out into the dark evening, shutting the door softly behind me. I looked up, tilting my head back, and stared up at the darkened dilapidated tower that I liked to call Kent's brooding place.

Whatever had gone down with Jen was surely what had brought

him here, if he was even up there. I'd bet tomorrow's breakfast that he was. I slowly made my way up the metal ladder to the top of the tower. I stared into the darkness when I reached the top, trying to make Kent's shape out from the rest of the shadows. The breeze that made the trees sway washed over me, and I shivered.

After my eyes adjusted I caught sight of his form. Right on the edge of the tower he sat with his legs dangling over the side. His tie was loose around his neck and his jacket was balled up and resting not far from him looking like a sleeping, disheveled cat. This is where he always came to clear his head. This was where he came to make his decisions and let his anger and frustrations out. I smiled as I remembered the first time he brought me up here. It was nice to have a decent memory regarding losing my virginity because the event itself had sucked so badly.

I stepped forward, coming up behind him slowly. My heels were the only sound aside from the wind which was still blowing past my ears.

"Don't jump. I would be devastated." I hoped my joke would land and sighed when I was unable to get a chuckle from him.

"Jumping is not the hard part, it's the landing at the bottom that sucks. Seconds of freedom and flying, and for what? Pain for the rest of your life? Shouldn't you be off having fun somewhere with Dave?" Kent hadn't looked back at me yet. "Why are you here?"

I sighed softly when I was unable to get a chuckle from him. I sat down beside him carefully. After a fall off a stripper pole a couple of years ago I developed a fear of heights. I dangled my legs over the edge too. I put my hands in my lap and stared at him, my head turned to the side.

"I ran into Jen. So I couldn't possibly have fun knowing that my best friend was probably very hurt because his wife returned his gift."

"If she would have bought that dress herself, she would have loved it." He shook his head and let out a defeated sigh. "I bought it for her and she decided it was too much. I should be able to buy my own wife a gift with the money I work so hard for." The muscles in his jaw worked as his teeth clenched together, a bit of anger showing through his usually calm facade.

"I think maybe she just wants your time," I clasped and unclasped my hands in my lap, unsure of how he would receive my feedback.

Kent nodded his head. "I know that's what she wants. We tried that already. I put one of the guys in charge of each place and I took time off. Without me being there though business was lacking and was dropping off. No people equals no money. Soon she was telling me I needed to be there. Now you can see why I'm such a fucking mess, Elly." Again his head shook back and forth. "We're not doing well, Elly. Not at all."

Kent may have given up but Jen didn't seem like she had just yet. It was up to me to push my friend to fight. He picked Jen as his first kiss, his first girlfriend, his first everything and I wasn't going to let his momentary anger over a dress cause him to do or say something that was going to jeopardize what he built his most of his life to accomplish.

"Maybe not now, but it's obvious that you both still want it to work out. And that's something, isn't it?" I hated seeing them like this. They both needed a push towards each other. Maybe counseling.

He turned his head and looked at me for a long moment. His eyes were red rimmed and it was obvious that he'd been crying.

"It's just hard, Elly. I work so hard to give her the things she obviously wants, but she just doesn't seem to enjoy it. I...I—," his words broke off as his gaze turned back out towards the city.

This was hard for me too. Seeing him in pain, wanting to comfort him, but refraining. I hadn't touched him for longer than thirty seconds since the night of his bachelor party.

"You're not happy and she's not happy," I swallowed the lump in my throat as I looked at his tear stained cheeks. "You need to do what will make you happy, Kent."

"I just don't want to think about work. I just want to play a video game or watch a movie," he shook his head. "I just want to have some fun for once instead of worrying about everything else."

"Then close your expansion stores and keep the most lucrative one open. Take your life back and let Jen know that X is how much money you're going to make. Then take time to play a video game or watch a movie." I sighed softly, the fight leaving me as quickly as it had come. "I work a lot too, Ken. Two jobs. But I still manage to find time for fun. I'm not sure that this is all her fault."

"I already told her I'd get rid of one and wouldn't open the other. She told me no. I've had offers on the business, but I've turned them down. I've tried, Elly. I have."

"It's your business, Kent. And it's your life. You need to stop letting her steamroll it, if that's what you feel she's doing here."

I watched him, letting him run what I'd said through his mind a little longer. I turned my attention to the city landscape, it all looked so small from up here. Perspective was everything. From my perspective Kent was tired of Jen being unhappy with everything he'd tried to give her. And Jen was tired of feeling alone in her marriage.

Kent sat there for a moment before he finally spoke up, "I got some Mountain Dew at the house and I DVRed an old scary movie. You game?"

I opened my mouth to accept right away but paused. What would Jen think if she came home and saw me with Kent watching a movie on their couch? Would she care? Was she allowed to care? I was just his friend. But I had told her that I was tired and needed to get home for my early shift tomorrow. And shouldn't Kent be spending this time with Jen to try and work things out?

"What about Jen? Shouldn't you ask her first? She also mentioned to me that she wanted to have some fun tonight. Maybe you two could spend some time together?"

He scoffed. "Then that means she was going to go out with her girlfriends. That means no dudes allowed. Sounds like that clears me to hang out with my best friends. Yeah?"

"....I have to get up early for work in the morning?" I had to try to use the same excuse on Kent as I did with Jen, at the very least. "You should call your other friends instead, like Mike or Paul..."

"It's been too long since I've hung out with you, Elly. Sometimes when you get pulled knee deep into life you forget the important things, like your real friends. I have to get up early too. I have some businesses to sell and some life to recapture. C'mon, I'll even sweeten the deal with a pedicure."

I hesitated. I had purposely not spent time alone with him in any setting outside of his office. My fatal mistake was looking him in the eye. Seeing the hope and desperation there, I couldn't resist any longer. I sighed and turned around, crawling a bit away from the edge before standing up.

"Fine. No toe nail painting, though." Even if I went over to his house, it didn't mean I had to have him touching me. It was basically the same thing as me touching him and it was a very non-platonic thing to do.

"What, don't paint your toenails anymore? You used to bug me about that all the time." Finally he chuckled as he pushed back from the edge and grabbed his jacket. He stood up and moved towards the ladder, waiting for me to join him. I closed the distance between us.

"That was back in high school. I pay someone to do it now," I hated lying to him but it was easier than the truth. I stood next to the ladder and looked down briefly. "You have to go first. If I fall I want you to be there to break it." I smiled innocently to him.

Chapter 5

Kent was starting to come out of his emotional funk.

"Alright, well I guess that will work. I'll make sure not to look up then Miss I'm-Wearing-A-Fancy-Skirt."

I knew he was being serious. He was always proper and gentlemanly, even when we were teenagers. But he probably was just like that with me because he saw me as a friend, like one of the dudes. If I didn't keep reminding myself of that I might let my old feelings resurface. They had to stay buried deep. I didn't want to be hurt like that again.

"You'd better not."

I waited for him to start down and then headed down behind him. Once he was halfway down I screamed, looking down to see if he was going to look up. When he looked up and spotted the black thong under my skirt he blushed, his cheeks burning with his embarrassment. I didn't get to see them for more than a second though before he was looking down at his feet, concentrating on the task at hand.

I grinned at my victory. "You owe me next week's allowance."

"Bah, playing on my chivalry to get money out of me. You never did play fair!" Kent chuckled as he reached the bottom and stepped back to wait for me to come down the rest of the way.

I huffed softly when my heel connected with the ground. "Oh, thank God, I made it! I wish you'd pick a less vertical spot to lick your wounds. Are you going to call the cab or do you want me to?" I already started pulling my phone from my purse, shivering as the wind sent a gust over us.

I felt something sliding over my shoulders. I gazed at the jacket that Kent was no longer wearing and looked at him, his tie was slightly blowing in the breeze.

"Call a cab? We could just walk. It isn't that far."

I pulled the jacket closed in the front and slipped my phone back into my purse. "Thanks. Let's go before my feet fall off."

We walked beside each other, untouching and then I heard him chortle. "Feet fall off. You want a ride?" He pointed to his back with his thumb. "First one's free, then you owe me lunch."

I laughed softly and shook my head, "No, thanks. I'll survive." What was with him wanting to touch me all of a sudden? He went from not even looking at me during dinner to wanting to grab my ass and call it a piggy-back ride. I mentally tried to count how many drinks he'd had. It hadn't been enough to make him drunk.

"Alright, then." He chuckled to himself as we moved on towards the house he shared with his wife. We went over idle small talk, like how my work was going, how he couldn't find anyone to manage a business and soon enough we were walking up the driveway to the large house.

I hadn't been over much except for the occasional dinner party where Jen tried to set me up with her few single male acquaintances. I smiled patiently as I waited for Kent to open the door. I entered the house and looked around, nodding. Everything was different.

"Jen has good taste."

"She's done all the decorating, as you know. I just pay for the stuff." He shut the door behind us. "Just toss the jacket on the coat rack if you want. I'll get us some Dew and meet you on the couch!" For the first time in a long while he seemed really excited, more like the Kent I'd known most of my life.

I put his jacket up as he'd instructed and then made my way into the living room. I sat down on the beautiful yet uncomfortable couch, pulling my shoes off slowly one by one. I let them drop to the floor and pulled my feet up under my skirt. I looked around in amazement. Their living room looked like something out of a decorating magazine. There was nothing but intentional clutter, beautiful art, and expensive furniture. No personal pictures, no dust. Nothing was out of place.

Kent came in the living room with two glasses of that sweet nectar also known as Mountain Dew. I couldn't drink the whole thing, I wasn't a sugar fiend anymore, but I accepted it as he held it out to me. "Thanks."

I smiled as I watched him take a seat next to me and pick up one of the many remotes that had been tucked away in a basket. He turned the TV on and then the DVR player. "I was going to watch it last night, but I didn't get around to it. But now... now it's gonna happen!" I laughed at his excitement. I only ever achieved that level of excitement these days when I was buying a new pair of shoes... or playing with my band.

"You sound like you did when you first watched the Spiderman movie. Your mom kept interrupting your scheduled movie time and it was a whole week before you got around to it, do you remember?" I took a small sip before placing it on the side table closest to me. Oh crap! I grabbed a coaster and lifted my glass, setting it carefully on top so that I wouldn't leave a mark.

"Yeah, I remember. You know Jen doesn't like scary movies? Every time she came in last night I had to cut it off." He drank half of his Dew before putting it aside as well, not bothering with a coaster. I didn't want to see Jen's reaction when she found out.

I stretched my arms overhead and then crossed them, holding myself.

"Oh, I almost forgot." Kent reached between his side of the couch and the side table and pulled out the awful yellow blanket that had been in his school-aged bedroom longer than I had. As he shook it out a pillow fell out onto the floor. He tried to shove it back between couch quickly and offered the blanket to me. "Here ya go."

I leaned forward to make sure I saw what I thought I'd seen and then leaned back, my eyebrow raised, "Have you been sleeping on the couch?"

Kent grimaced as he picked up the Dew and took a drink.

"Yeah," he said. He took one more drink and returned it to the table by the couch. His eyes were focused on the TV. If he wanted to avoid my questioning stares that was fine by me. I'd still get my answers.

I stared at the TV too and tried to remain casual, "Because you're just so tired when you come home or...?"

"Because Jen and I haven't slept in the same bed in over a month."

I was stunned. Firstly, because it was so easy to get that information out of him and secondly, because he had been sleeping on a couch for a whole month and hadn't told me. I tried not to let my disbelief show. I busied myself by tucking the blanket around me.

"But I mean...It's a big house, why not sleep in one of the other bedrooms?"

His scent slowly surrounded my senses and I tried to resist inhaling deeply. I kept reminding myself it was because his scent was associated with so many memories, it had nothing to do with those old feelings I used to have for him.

"Because it doesn't feel right sleeping in a bed alone is all. I'd much rather crash the couch."

"It's good to know you can sleep just about anywhere...except a—"

A gangly hand popped out unexpectedly and I screamed, covering my face with the blanket. I heard him laugh at me and uncovered my face enough to glare at him.

"You scaredy cat." He casually put his arm around my shoulder and I felt my body tense. "Are you always gonna get scared at the wittle scawry movies?" He teased me as he turned his attention back to the TV.

"Um, yes...I have good survival instincts, that's all. I'll be right back."

I got up off the couch and went to the bathroom. I took the next few minutes to splash some water on my face and try to figure out why I was feeling so weird. It was Kent, he was just being Kent. He was being casual and friendly. There was nothing behind it, never would be.

I looked at myself in the mirror, pointed at my nose and whispered, "Stop being ridiculous! Stop conjuring up fiction in your silly head, Elly. Be. A. Good. Friend."

I exhaled quickly, smoothed out my dress and then left the bathroom. I was only gone for a few minutes before coming back. I pulled the blanket around myself again and stared at the TV as the zombie with the gnarly hand chased a half-naked, big-boobed girl down the street.

The movie was half over and I whispered, pulling the blanket up to my nose, "They're all gonna die..."

"You know how these movies generally work. Most of the time yes, they do." Kent covered a yawn with his fist.

"I always hope they live," I whispered again. I grabbed the blanket from my shoulders and tucked it around him. He looked so tired and so sad. My heart was hurting for him and his marriage woes. "Looks like it's getting close to your bedtime."

"I got enough to finish the movie! I'm not passing out yet, Elly.

Don't forget who usually won those late night gaming sessions! It was me because you always passed out."

I rolled my eyes and shook my head. "Yeah, but you're getting old. You don't party long into the night like I do." I grinned as I tucked my hands into the crooks of my elbows and snuggled back against the couch.

"Yeah, whatever. I can run laps around you any day of the week." He chuckled and pushed part of the blanket onto me. "Just try to finish the movie without screaming again and then we'll call it a night. Alright?"

"I don't remember you being so bossy. Being your own boss must have done that to you, BossyPants." I pushed the blanket back onto him.

"I'm gonna wrap you up like a burrito if you don't accept my hospitality in my own house!"

He stuck his tongue out at me and then he flinched and gasped as the zombie attacked the half naked girl unexpectedly while she was finding comfort in the arms of her male counterpart. Kent was blushing as he glowered at me.

I pointed at him, hiding my giggles behind my hand. "What were you saying, Scaredy Kent?"

Kent grabbed the edge of the blanket and twirled it around us and tied it in a knot.

"Yeah, so what. It's a good movie if it gets me to jump! At least I'm not screaming."

I struggled against the blanket and sighed in defeat after a moment of trying to wiggle out of it. The whole right side of my body was touching his and I was reminded at how warm he was. "There is nothing wrong with screaming. God, you're like a bonfire."

"Screaming makes the blood move. As far as being a furnace... yes, I am. I can only sleep with a sheet year round."

Kent didn't seem to think much about our contact. It was all I could think about, him wrapping me up like he used to when we were teenagers, his lips kissing my shoulder, unlike when we were teenagers... I hopped in my seat because of the movie, but held back my scream.

"I think you forget I've known you since before you could walk," I countered.

"I know. You forget how hot my body runs in temperature? You don't remember complaining about being cold in my room and I'm running around in shorts and a t-shirt? Elly..." he sounded disappointed.

I laughed. "Kent..." And then I rolled my eyes, "If I think about it, yes, I remember. But when I think about Kent, my friend, that doesn't usually pop up." Not that specifically. Other things popped up, but not him running around in shorts all the time.

There was a raise of his eyebrow. "Oh yeah? Maybe I've forgotten but you seem to be holding something over my head. Tell me."

I shook my head, "Nothing, I don't think. It's just that when I think of you I just think of nerdy you with glasses and those awful 90's clothes...and a morbid fear of girls." Of wanting to kiss you so hard that your glasses would fall off. And all those nights I'd prayed that you'd notice the parts of me that were round in a sexy, womanly way and not just in your sleep or in a drunken stupor. I kept those thoughts in my head.

"Right. Not Kent who got tired of being picked on and started working out and got rid of the glasses," he frowned, "And I didn't have a fear of girls, just a healthy weariness of them."

"I don't think about how cold your room used to be or all the crusty socks under your bed either..." I bit my lower lip to keep from grinning too wide. His reaction was going to be classic.

He blinked, "When were you looking under my bed!"

My smiled dropped. His face was turning red.

"Well, did you ever wear those frilly pink panties with the bows on them?" he raised his eyebrow, "Yeah, I knew about those. They were sitting on top of your dresser one day when I came over and I pretended not to see them so you wouldn't be embarrassed."

I had an exact idea about what panties he was talking about. I'd bought them on the very off chance that I could get Kent into my plus-sized jeans. I laughed and gasped, pointing at him accusingly.

"I knew you saw them. I was wondering when you'd say

something about them. I wear panties like that all the time." I stuck my tongue out at him and wondered if he was going to try to lift up my skirt to see. I scolded myself for even thinking about it.

Kent chuckled. "The good ol'days, right Elly?" For a moment he didn't say anything. "I miss this. I know we're both really busy, but why did we stop hanging out so much?"

Because of Jen. I cleared my throat and reached out from the blanket, grabbing my phone. "It's late, Kent, I should get going..." I wouldn't meet his gaze, I didn't want him to see what was in my eyes. The regret, the guilt for being so jealous, the hurt he'd put there when he'd chosen her over me so many times in the past.

Kent was about ready to say something but something caught his eye and he looked behind me. In the doorway stood Jen, staring at us. Her purse dangled in her hand, her eyelids wide with disbelief, "What the hell is going on here?"

Ken pushed the blanket aside and stood up. "We were just catching up. It's nothing to worry about, Jen."

Jen, however, was more than worried. She was livid. "In our own house, Kent? You'd bring her here to do that?" We could smell the liquor on her breath from across the room.

I stood up quickly and tried to change the subject, "Jen, did you have a good time?" I approached Jen steadily, acting like the innocent party that I was, a smile on my lips.

Jen glared at me. Her eyes were so full of anger and rage that it was actually frightening. My mouth went dry.

"Get out," she spat at me.

Kent approached the two of us from behind, his arms out to embrace his wife. "Jen, calm down. This isn't what you think."

"Kent, she's right. It's late. We all need some rest." I retreated, grabbing my shoes and purse before anything was said that couldn't be forgiven.

"Good night, Elly." It was the last thing that was said to me before I walked out the large door. As I walked away from the house I could hear Jen yelling at him. As I neared the bottom of the driveway I heard Kent fire back, his temper officially lost.

I considered going back but it wasn't my fight, it was theirs. As much as I wanted to protect and defend Kent, it wasn't my place. I put my shoes on and walked down the street, pulling out my phone to call for a cab and text with Stacy as I waited for it to arrive.

> ME: HOLY SHIT! I THINK I MAY HAVE JUST BURNED DOWN KENT'S HOUSE.

> STACY: WHAT?? YOU BURNED DOWN HIS HOUSE? WHAT DID HE DO?

> ME: I MEANT HIS ... NOT HIS REAL ONE. HIS MARRIAGE HOUSE. THEY ARE FIGHTING FIERCELY IN THERE.

> STACY: OH. I ALMOST PEED MY PANTS. DON'T DO THAT TO A SISTA.

I shivered as the wind battered me some more.

> ME: SHIT IT'S COLD OUT HERE. AND DARK... LIONS, AND TIGERS, AND BEARS...

> STACY: OH MY! HAHA. STOP IT. SERIOUSLY, WHAT DID YOU DO? DID YOU KISS HIM??

> ME: OMG, NO! HE WAS POUTING ABOUT JEN RETURNING HIS PRESENT SO I AGREED TO WATCH A MOVIE WITH HIM. JEN CAME HOME AND WAS PISSED ABOUT IT.

> STACY: UGH. SERIOUSLY? SHE'S SERIOUSLY INSECURE. YOU SHOULD'VE KISSED HIM.

> ME: STACY! OMG!!! I'M NOT KISSING KENT AND WILL NOT. NEVER AGAIN. HE'S LIKE THE TRIPLE CHOCOLATE TOWER AT GUPPY'S. IT LOOKS REALLY GOOD, TASTES REALLY GOOD FOR THE MOMENT, BUT ONCE IT SETTLES YOU REGRET IT IMMEDIATELY AND YOU NEVER WANT TO EAT IT AGAIN.

> STACY: ... KEEP TELLING YOURSELF THAT.

The cab pulled up to the curb and I said goodnight to Stacy. I looked at their house as I was driven away. It looked picture perfect on the outside.

This is the end of your Old Friends Preview. Go to your book retailer to order the next in the series to read Elly and Kent's Happily Ever After.

#JustFriends Series

Just Friends - Elly & Kent
Old Friends - Elly & Kent HEA
Fast Friends - Rio & Stacy
Secret Friends - James & Ainsley

Other Novels By Marie Cole

Taming the Viking
(Historical Romance)

The Beginning of Always
(Mythology Romance)

If you want to delve deeper into the world of Elly and Kent be sure to sign up for Marie's newsletter. As a thank you for subscribing she'll send you a copy of HS Friends [Elly and Kent's high school experiences] absolutely free! You've got nothing to lose.

Go to **www.mariecolebooks.com** to sign up today.

Printed in Great Britain
by Amazon